THE SEED

DAVIDE DE ANGELIS

THE SEED
Davide De Angelis

Published by Creation Books 2004
www.creationbooks.com

Cover painting by Davide De Angelis
Back cover drawing and visual segues by Davide De Angelis

Edited by Esther De Angelis

ISBN 1-84068-114-4

THE SEED

I remember the Teachers, Writers, Musicians and Artists who have flowed through my mind and become part of 'The Mix' that is now The Seed. Their words, sounds and images have taken me to places - away from the monochrome - where a different, more vibrant alchemy is lived and played. Their gifts can all be found in The Seed::::in a glance ~ a deed ~ a flash of colour in the midst of some fast, streaming action. In this sense The Seed is a Collaboration ~ an Event ~ a Thought-Sampler that celebrates the interconnectedness of life.

Major respect to Creation Books for their commitment to creativity and experiment.

Gratitude flows abundantly to Esther De Angelis ~ the creative force who transformed The Seed with her passion and inspiring ideas.

Respect to Neil Henderson.

The Seed is dedicated to Sylvia and Rolando ~ may you journey to the land where we walk without footprints.

The taste of death is less bitter than 'life' without ending. In the stream, which bleeds from the emerald silence of eternity, you will forget and again seek the illusion of time. It is then that the endless moment is lost and you must breathe again. And if nothing ever comes to lift you from the damp earth and walk you back into the light, then you will truly sleep as never before.

The Seed Singer

1

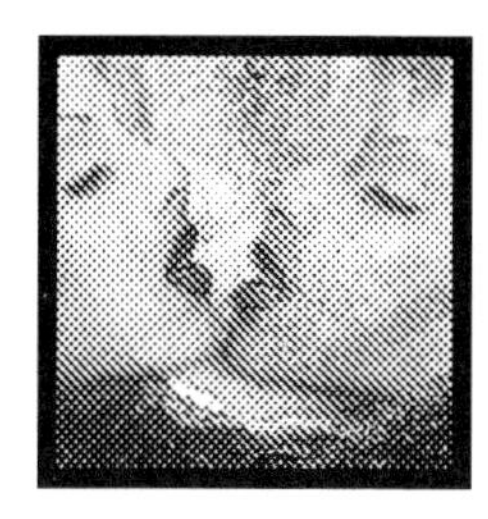

vivid images in a mind ~

sound ~

movement..........

Stepping through clouds of sepia-flecked voices, Dreamweaver moved as a soft breath through the luminous spirit-glimmer of his dream. He was journeying to find Sunixlan, the Dream-Shaman. Before crossing the divide, he had meticulously constructed a powerful dream-body: a rhythmic, feeling simile, manifest only where his thoughts touched it.

He stopped to check his progress. There was uneasiness simmering, something stroking the energy that glued this dream together. Awareness echoed in the distance, demanding that he wake himself. He'd made this journey countless times; impatient, he ignored its call.

As Dreamweaver looked ahead, singing shadows dripped from his eyes twisting into the trunks and branches of a forest. He watched the thrust of succulents out of raw earth, the burst of gleaming waxed flora. He smelt the rotting of age, the pungency of swelling fruits and heard the shrill of a fly's wings. For an instant, the organics of death and ceaseless birth washed through him.

A song began to snake its way through the trees, crisp notes formed a powerful woman's voice. He moved and the song kept pace with his steps. He caught sight of her purple robe, the flowing tresses of her moonlight hair. Although he couldn't see the details of her face, the force of her presence compelled him to follow her. Her song unwound like the supplest of vines, its mystery making her delicious.

The tune filled his mind as it opened to leave words he could understand.

'Sunixlan cannot bring you the energy to finish your story,' she sang.

Dreamweaver's body shook with the impact of her words. A violent shiver bled upwards from the base of his spine. He tried to center himself before hastily following her movements through the trees.

Now fueled by a mix of arousal and fear, he continued after her. Her face remained hidden in a blur of forest colours.

Playful laughter drifted through the leaves. 'I have sent the Dream-Shaman away: there is knowledge that he needs to acquire.'

'What knowledge...who are you to command him?' Demanded Dreamweaver.

Suddenly, the desiccation of death filled his nostrils.

She slowed. 'Yes, he has no more time for stories,' she sang 'you're beginning to understand this dream. You will see how much of the brilliance you crave is created from what Sunixlan missed. You will mourn his departure though.'

Dreamweaver began running towards her, but despite his agility, he couldn't draw closer. What was she? He must touch her! Everything else was pushed to the side as the boiling milk of life ran through him. Jagged branches gashed his face. Spores clogged his eyes and stung his throat. He must have her!

'Strength has deserted you, Dreamweaver,' she sang as she flew like a wisp into the dark depths of the forest and vanished.

Stumbling, he crashed face down into the thicket, the thud of flesh meeting stone. Darkness descended in an instant, a thick, impenetrable shroud. There were creatures around him, accompanied by the blurred hum of nervous flappings. He was deserted and blind. The awareness that he was dreaming, now a tiny stain in the distance.

The darkness swelled with the low chanting of women's voices, a vibrant unceasing hum.

Gasping for breath, the laconic charge of coital still called, he tasted its flavour on his tongue. His mind teamed with dissolute thoughts: the seeing touch of love-soaked fingers: dreadful words that came as children weeping: the knowing eyes of Sunixlan.

Sickly sweat drenched his flesh. It seeped through his clothes. There is no meaning in this, he thought, no meaning in me. The thought seemed to arrive from nowhere. It chilled him to the bone.

Slowly, he dragged himself up, trembling. His heart pounding fit to burst. Stretching out his arms, he grasped at the edges of darkness revealing the shape of a woman. She was swathed in a silken cloth of intricate threads. His bloodied hands passed nervously over her sleek form, the sinews strong and deep in the flesh. He pulled her close and laid his cheek on her breast, wetting her with tears and the saliva from his mouth. He bathed like a child in the vital juice of her essence.

'You have discovered what lurks behind all illusions,' she sang softly. 'Not a single thing, in all the realms, has any meaning: no thought, no experience, no form. Everything is empty. This hidden truth is the root of all fear.'

She paused briefly before continuing. 'In your world it is the purpose of the Storytellers to disguise this terrifying void. Your words paint images onto thoughts and people perceive them as meaningful.'

Her hand smoothed his damp hair. 'Never forget, all worlds are sightless. 'Seeing' can only be imagined. Your new eyes are beginning to open and you are searching for a story to test your powers. You're searching for words that paint 'nothing' with such passion as to bring it fully alive. To finally be the illusionist in perfect harmony with the illusion.'

Suddenly, Dreamweaver's impulse was to turn and run, sickness oozed upwards from his stomach, excitement struggled with revulsion. She had found an unknown feeling coiled in his being and awoken it. It was potent, sure of itself and cried out to be satisfied. In that instant, it threatened to overpower him, to tear him open and take birth. He tried desperately to pull away, to see her face, but she held him in a vice-like grip. This is the illusion, he suddenly thought, I must find Sunixlan and finish the story.

'I wil...fin...,' he tried to speak, swallowing hard, fighting off waves of nausea.

The sticky fermented smell of the Dream-Shaman's elixir filled his nostrils. The bitter taste slicked across his tongue, the energy of words carrying eyes deep into his throat. Down deep within his dream-body, deep within himself, into the molten blood of a new world filled with synovial creatures.

Finally, words coated in dream-power began to solidify. He felt the essence and form of story, the pulse of syntax. The darkness fled and he was flooded with images.

He began speaking in a strong moist voice.

With the Ghost-Witch and Sunixlan by my side, I entered the enchanted land ruled by MindJadium. He was the most powerful sorcerer the realm of dreams had ever known. He made medicine from the smoke of mind and created beasts from fire and thought.

It was a land of healing and beauty.

Feel him now in your own smoke.... feel him...

In a shocking slur, Dreamweaver's voice transformed. Strange sounds filled his mind. The visible mathematics of their genius blazed from his lips like spectres. For an instant, he thought these new words would eat him alive. His entire being smoldered with excitement.

What power was contained in these words? He would explore this power, shape this power.

A drak and terirlbe frcoe had teakn pesisososn of the sorcerer MindJadium ~ through streams of chaos, the Ghost-Witch pulled me into a swarm of Black Light

She turned her gaze to Sunixlan, but the Dream-Shaman was already crawling with MindJadium's deadly Lucid.

'Darkness…!' gasped Sunixlan. 'Take me into your arms.' And with all his strength, he placed a Trance-Weapon into his mouth, ready to chant his deadly mantra.

Faster than light, MindJadium shaped his words into a strange and thoughtless sound that swept like velvet through Sunixlan's skull. The Dream-Shaman grasped his last gleaming visual, as burning words flew useless from the Trance-Weapon

As we dropped into the Black Light, I looked back and saw the image of Sunixlan's magical form encased in a cloud of nightmares. Tiny, gleaming ghosts penetrating his brilliant aura, erasing him from the dream.

Sunixlan drank in his destruction like flowing spring water. The gauzy remnant of his dazling presence embraced my eyes, the after-glow of his face was strong, passionate and calm.

Instinct drew me towards him.

'Leave him, Dreamweaver!' insisted the Ghost-Witch, pulling me down into the spume of dreams. She knew exactly what I was thinking. Back in the realm of time, blood and breath would have no appetite to give him new life.

'It's too late for him,' she cried, 'there's nothing we can do.'

Dreamweaver lived the words. He felt them surging through his blood. Somehow they were part of him. He watched them taking shape; the violence unfolding.

'He must have known it was oblivion to try and chant the mantra into MindJadium,' I shouted.

'Sunixlan knew it was the only way to give you a chance, Dreamweaver!' screamed the Ghost-Witch. 'Only you know the ultimate words to destroy him.'

'Hell! I can't find them!'

Suddenly, MindJadium appeared, hovering above us. The enchantment of his beautified dream-flesh was bleached to a deadly white. His fierce, exotic features smoldered with sensual static.

Possessed by the terrible force, he tore at his own body. He spat and thrashed. Waves of howling nightmares poured from his skin. Staggering from this carnage, his fine coating of illusion hung screaming in tatters.

'I will destroy you all....!' He yelled, his voice plunging to deep baritone slabs. 'I shall destroy the very essence of life!!'

He turned his penetrating eyes towards the Black Light. 'I.....will... speak the...destruction....' His voice faltered.

With that he tore a Light-Demon from his eyes. It floated above him like a satellite, its ghostly machine hypnotising the air with hatred. It searched for the words that lay buried in my soul. The words I could not utter. It licked at their power.

The words gushed from Dreamweaver's lips, He was shaping a new world. It was impossible to describe the sensations they awoke in him. They exploded into being, glittered like shattering glass. He let them come...

The throb of terror gripped my mind. How could this happen? The beauty, the healing? What has MindJadium become?

The Ghost-Witch pulled me closer until we were locked like lovers. Her grip tightened around my arms and the ground beneath our feet rippled with MindJadium's anger. We stared into his lethal dynamics.

'Even like this he's still magnificent,' whispered the Ghost-Witch.

We are lost, destroyed...I thought.

MindJadium was defaced, scrawled with entropy. His dream-flesh was no longer healing instantaneously. Whole sheets floated weightlessly from his image, crumbling like ancient plasterwork.

Now, he moved forward firing nightmares from each hand and

chanting through a smoldering Trance-Weapon.

(((STEMOLD^UT^ENTIMON^STEMOLD^UT^ENTIMON)))

The sound scorched my soul, like spiritual napalm.

MindJadium smiled arrogantly.

'The healing energy you seek to take back to your world...can never...be released without...MY power, Dreamweaver,' he choked. The ground liquefied beneath his feet. 'It's...over...and you will... never...leave here. No healing will ever leave here again.'

The sky was filled with MindJadium's terrible drone. Swirling darkness enveloped the land from hemisphere to hemisphere. Clouds of Dream-Spirits appeared and desperately beamed light from their eyes, throwing it across the skies. It spread through the action in bright~monochrome~strobes.

At once, MindJadium's Light-Demon swooped down in rhythmic slow motion, searching us out. I managed to shield the Ghost-Witch from its lethal words. My mind was fighting the supernova coursing through my head. Everything was possessed by MindJadium's poltergeistic genius, tearing at this realm's hypnotic underpinning, pulling us apart:::::

A second wave of destruction surged forth from the Light-Demon's lips. This time its twisted syntax engorged the Ghost-Witch, sending swirls of dark energy shooting through her body. The impact blasted me out of the Black Light, as Mindjadium howled with sickening laughter.

I lay motionless, in agony, begging his eternal darkness to arrive.

Robbed of dream-force, thoughts blundered through my mind, but were whipped away before any picture could give them meaning. I groped blindly for the Ghost-Witch.

Her voice cried out... 'Dreamweaver!... Find me Dreamweaver... save me from the darkness.'

Her screams faded into the void and she was gone.

I was beyond fear or hope now, beyond dreams and all that I'd ever desired. Another thunder-kissed word struck the ground beside me – huge – blinding. I tried to move, but the will to exist had deserted me. I slid lifelessly towards MindJadium's glistening destruction.

I stared up at him bewildered and exhausted. My hand ran across the Ghost-Witch's discarded Trance-Weapon. A thought lingered in the distance...'Finish it!'

Then MindJadium laughed, but now the sound flowed easily like a fresh morning breeze. He was transformed, torment vanished. The terrible force somehow vanquished.

He floated down to stand beside me. In a soft voice he said: 'It's already finished, Dreamweaver. The story you brought to this blessed land will end here.'

There was no more time in his eyes. For a moment a spasm of dry sobbing shook me. A clap of thunder ran across the barren sky and faded away.

'It is done,' he said, 'I forgive you, Dreamweaver.' He looked down. 'Forgiveness turns misery into glory. What is past will cast no shadow to darken the present.'

He smoldered like a stick of pernicious incense, his once spell-binding face was a mask of shadows. But I saw such beauty in his condition, no conflict, reality withdrawing from illusion.

'Now you will remember the chant for me, Dreamweaver,' he said, 'and you will send it through me.'

He knelt down and gently placed his Trance-Weapon against my mouth. 'Do it now,' he whispered.

As the chant entered, he flew back from me. A swirling mist from his mouth took shape as ghostly women with trailing garments. A rippling scream seized his intricate being, cold as inverted love.

It rose up from his groin and out through the top of his head. The gaunt artistry of MindJadium's ravaged face was cremated in a heartbeat, his eyes twisted into spirals of frozen flame. Everything was pulled towards this ending. Nothing was spared its seduction.

A painful constriction gripped the Dream World. Shadows fled from their makers to hide in thinking ghosts. They rolled and twisted through sheets of melting visions. Where MindJadium had been, there now stood a pillar of flames, a missile roaring at the sky. It gave off a hideous light which chased and devoured every fleeing personae.

The earth sucked me down into a dark dreamless machine. Thoughts became blurred strokes and faded away into a dense embracing silence where nothing was left to think or feel or be.....

>>> Everything froze <<<

'No!' Screamed Dreamweaver. 'This cannot be my story...my images...'

He staggered to his feet, still tasting the remnants of Sunixlan's elixir. There was a wash of green. Everything was bathed in a rose-coloured pink, hinting a distant dawn. There was the moisture of dew clinging to his body, wrapping him in its silver cloak.

He studied his hands: no blood. His dream-body was strong and intact, free of pain.

In the distance, the woman's voice floated forward like a mist. Dreamweaver breathed in her song

His eyes flashed.

'Very good...very good,' she sang softly. 'You've suffered, Dreamweaver. You've felt a new way of telling. Now you are not afraid to make other things suffer with your words. You understand the true power of stories. You see clearly all worlds are made of stories not atoms. And you have just destroyed a whole world.'

Dreamweaver remained quite still, resisting the temptation to follow the voice again. His words had stripped away the veil of Storytellers'

Law to reveal a secret just beyond his reach. Like a memory bleeding through amnesia the secret hovered seductively...somewhere.

Her song wafted through. 'Many years ago when the gift of dreams first came, you made a pact with limitation. It was not your fault, you were just a child. Now you sense that error, but cannot place its source, it constantly gnaws at your soul.'

The song became softer. 'Your stories shimmer for a brief moment in the dreamless minds; they come alive through them, yet ultimately they fade away. You're so tired of those dream-words, and your life is trapped inside their anaemic flesh.'

'Why did the world stop dreaming…do you know why?' Asked, Dreamweaver.

She didn't answer his question. 'There is a sacred place on Earth that you must find, Dreamweaver,' she sang. 'There is a story waiting to be told.'

Dreamweaver peered into the forest. A soft breeze brushed his face. Then, he felt the fingers of his right hand were still twisted around the icy precision of the Ghost-Witch's Trance-Weapon. His mind sharpened, remembering his last actions in the story. With machine-like purpose he drew the weapon up, placing it between his teeth.

The brightness of morning suddenly failed, as a great black cloud sailed across the sky. An ear-piercing scream filled the air, so wild, so despairing that everything cowered.

Dreamweaver's eyes glazed over as his mouth closed around the weapon. He spoke the word (((OBLIVION))).

An instant of pain registered on his face.

Then he saw nothing – thought nothing>>>>>>>>>

>>> Darkness – Silence <<<

2

Deken Nos-Antimon, known to the *'dreamless'* world as Dreamweaver, wrenched the tiny, spinning Mer-Ka-Ba from his mouth and hurled it across the room. Beads of sweat poured downs his face as his eyes sprung open, clouded with pain. His mind searched for thoughts.

Sunlight blazed through a large, uneven window at the far end of the room, gilding the heavy dust motes and splintering into millions of golden shards as it struck his face. The room was curved and inviting, fashioned by hand from earth and water. The walls were white and velvety like the flesh of a large soft animal. Bright ochre rugs covered the floor, each one populated by crude, unrealised figures. Everything about them seemed incongruous and ill conceived, as if their creator had little understanding of form or beauty. At the far end there stood a single wooden desk laden with Word~Vessels that chattered in a sleepy, hypnotic static.

'Is the story finished?' came a gentle, feminine voice from behind.

It was dangerous to disturb a Storyteller on a Dream-Journey, and Dreamweaver swung round angrily and glared into the face of a young woman. Her slim, dark features composed, eyes sharp with concern.

'Go! leave me!' He snapped impatiently. 'Who let you past security?'

'Please don't be angry with me,' she pleaded. 'I'm so worried. They say you're possessed by something evil, they say you must leave now, and that we must mourn.' She bit into her bottom lip. 'You've made enemies, Deken, powerful enemies. They don't like what you're saying, and the other Storytellers grow restless.'

'You knew it was close,' he said studying her face. 'The stories don't fit my mind anymore. I must change everything, escape this stifling comfort. That is why I sent you away. I cannot share this with you.'

'I don't want to hear you say that!' she screamed, covering her ears. Your gift has made you arogant and selfish. They say you will die in the wilderness, or be killed by the Dreamless Elders before you even set foot outside the city. Do you think Death will ask your permission first?'

She moved over to the window. 'Look at them, what are they waiting for? Every day more come. Look at them, all they do is just sit and wait to touch you as you leave.' She laughed exhaustively. 'Damn you Deken Nos-Antimon, look at them.'

'Come away from the window. They're just people, not so very different from me. They cannot dream, but they believe, and sometimes I envy such blind faith.'

He plucked a Word~Vessel from his desk and held it up to the light. 'I have to go. You must understand. I can't flow with this tide anymore!'

'I understand,' she said sadly. 'I understand that it is you who have become blind. In seeking this elusive truth of yours, I sense you are in great danger. You refuse to tell your stories, yet you give the people no logical explanation. Don't you see Deken, your stories and the stories of the other gifted ones are their dreams – our dreams. Through your words we see into another realm, we see what we may one day become. You give us hope of what the human spirit can unfold from the mystery of life.'

'Look around you at what the Storytellers are creating, and tell me about the mystery of life. It is all based on error. Entertainment masquerading as wisdom.'

She pressed her argument. 'We search for our image, our lost presence in your stories. Shut out from the realm of dreams, we search for any vestige of our lost dream-self. In your words we can begin to recognise something magical that was once the gift of all humans. And in that magic, we can begin to heal.'

She looked away. 'You must continue. They won't let you jeopardise the work of the Storytellers. There is too much at stake.'

'I will find a way past them,' he said.

She looked down.

He slowly moved close to her. 'I don't understand what is happening to me,' he said, gently lifting her chin to look into her eyes. 'The Storytellers will brand me as something dangerous, but it is your choice, you decide if I am Healer or a Demon.'

He bent down and kissed the nape of her neck.

She closed her eyes. 'Demon,' she said.

He moved to pull away, but she immediately pulled him closer.

'Healer,' she said quickly. 'This time...'

At last she let go and he moved back. She kept her eyes closed and said, 'You are gone my Dreamweaver.'

'Gone,' he said…

3

A perfect circle lay etched in the dark, carbonised earth of a long forgotten land. Inside the circle there lay a strange, liminal geometry where things were not irrevocably fixed by the laws of matter. Dark lines fed from its core in raw, bestial scribbles that screamed in percussive chaos. They were mystifying, feverish, and bursting with unknown dangers. They sparkled moltenly in the slanted sun.

Dreamweaver placed his feet on the edge of the circle, resisting the temptation to gaze downwards and become lost in its patterns. He understood this was the end of a vast quest. But he could feel something unimaginable at this boundary which made him hesitate.

So it was true, he said to himself… *so it was true*.

He felt hidden forces watching him, unseen hands clutching at his body. Fear plucked at him, whispering through his cells. Succumb to the circle and you'll be lost to the world that hangs on your words. In that instant, the world seemed to stick to his mind as if it loved him. It told him it loved him too much to ever let him go.

He wasn't that easily fooled. He lived in a strange and difficult world. A world shaped by the shibboleth of a New Age for humanity: the Dreamless Time.

At first, the absence of dreams passed almost unnoticed except by intuitives, shamans and those versed in the wisdom of seers. That was until children across the world had begun to stop playing, interacting in the way that had sustained our evolution since the distant encryption of the human mind.

Everyone had watched helplessly as their children stared out at a world that bemused and terrified them. The hidden sting of this Dreamless Time, was the systematic loss of the ability to construct stories, to fundamentally create new ways of defining who and what we are in space and time.

Then, the complex wonder of human systems began to implode into chaos. Mass panic and violence spread like a biting wind across land, sea and air. Nations played out this strange, ritualistic act with impeccable technique. Angry fingers pointed across the Four Corners of the globe.

Huge swathes were convinced it was all some virulent super-virus concocted by providence, payment in kind for our poor custodianship of the Earth and her creatures. Still greater swathes believed it the work of a new type of nerve gas, spread by silent, shadow-like terrorists to ignite the final, devastating jihad.

Yet eerily, in the midst of the turmoil, it was as if everyone had always known that humanity would eventually become allergic to itself. These swirling reactions soon gave way to a deep, numbing sadness that carried no accusation. Humanity was at last united…united in grief.

This one seemingly unimportant ingredient removed from the recipe of creation had left the miraculous spectrum of human imagination faded like some ancient papyrus. Only in its loss was dreaming understood to be the most powerful microscope, the most powerful telescope, and the most powerful screen. Only in its loss was it understood that every power in human culture had its roots in 'Dream Power'.

Through dreams we entered into sacred space and time, travelled through gateways to bring back energies that coloured waking reality. This was how healers found their medicine, scientists their formulas, how great composers tapped into the stream of genius. This was where all stories gestated before entering thoughts and shaping the world.

But in the cloud of this new Dark Age, a few were born with the gift of dreams. And with the ripening of adulthood these sparkling morphogenes developed the capacity of full, lucid dreaming.

Equally divided between men and women of different race, the crowning glory blossomed fully, as each developed the power to temporarily re-ignite the mystery of dreams and imagination through the telling of amazing stories.

Their agile minds pulled resonance directly from the realm of dreams. They spoke in the magical, super-sentient syntax of Dream-Shamans. They were treasured by the world, Avatars sent to reawaken the miracle of human imagination.

Dreamweaver possessed this sacred tongue – spoke these stories - bound colour and image to monochromed minds; pulled hope from despair. The people suckled on his voice like new-born calves. He charged their blood with new energies.

His lips dripped with mesmerising tales plucked from a flowering mystery. Words became myths made out of never-thought memories and never-touched flesh. Each crafted tale was a dye that seeped into the mind to conjure new spectra.

He could turn effortlessly from the fecundity of a birthing goddess to the terrifying speed of an angry wind. From the nefarious thoughts of a jealous lover, to the quivering lustre of an insect's wing.

His words exposed sensuousness in sorrow and lies hidden in truth.

Dreamweaver's image was as vivid as his stories. Dark sheets of hair fell towards his waist, framing a bronze, delicately boned face - almost fragile - that seemed still in the process of construction. Large brown eyes peered from their sockets like spheres of shining alabaster.

He wore a face that was like a mask made from a collection of clever contradictions. A chin brushed with one of those *almost* beards, giving the impression of a rakish youth not yet matured. Although he had seen no more than thirty summers, he appeared scarred and lined by the thoughts and passions of a man who has felt innumerable sorrow.

He almost looked deliberately flawed for effect, disguising a sensuality that might turn a beast into a god.

As if to continue the enigma, his body was pared to a perfect whiplash, more like uncut crystal than muscle and sinew, and it was impossible to say if extreme martial practice or some clever genetic trick had achieved such an effect.

Rejecting the status of a Storyteller, in the wake of his departure, he'd reduced himself to a barely visible voyager. The untamed world soon grimed his manicured aura. In the dust-soaked planes his strong, intelligent clothes groped at his body in tatters.

On the avaricious streets of cities, they had meant something, but in the lonely wilderness, their flapping threads melded into a dream. They became creatures floating in his imagination to distract him from hunger and pain. Fatigue had interloped his mind, reduced him to thoughts that morphed into flesh, walked across fire, and slept in the sky.

The people had understood he needed to go, but while he was still present they'd pretended he would never leave and it would never end. Now as he stood in the scalding scrub, the hysterical tears of devoted followers, the kindly smile of his mother and the haunting sound of women keening his departure, grew dim.

What compulsion had moved him towards a threshold where the scrim between life and death was little more than shimmer, and what fragments lay in his mind like a fever-dream that he couldn't wake from?

Dreamweaver shared his gift with all the people, from criminals to kings. He was the most controversial of all the Storytellers, paying little attention to the restricting protocols that clung to his status. Yet in the stream of his wayward psyche, there now lurked something enticing and alien that he couldn't understand.

His dreams were now embalmed with a volatile, feminine presence, and he knew with unshakeable certainty that she was not from his own cache of characters. Like a brilliantly conceived virus, she had infiltrated his dreams, destroyed his Dream-Shaman and exposed a new method of storytelling. In her presence, his words exploded - vivid, sensual and delinquently unstable. Her etherial fingers caressed his molecules, a ghost-wave searching for feelings.

When he sat deep in trance, her strange songs formed into words and surged through his lips like a vast, marauding sermon. His own stories became entwined in her presence, calling him away, guiding him across the earth's multitude like a psychic radar, throwing him to the wilderness, enticing him into her Sacred Circle.

Dreamweaver moved on the edge of the Circle, his face was taut and the wind hit it like a fist. Small flies darted across the earth as scorpions danced and killed in the scrub. His only witnesses, insects and the wind.

Swirls of dust spiralled away as if they feared the Circle. Run, they cried, leave before it's too late. The wind grew stronger, and tore branches from small, brittle trees hurling them across the earth like a poltergeist. *The time has arrived*, he thought. He slowly closed his wind-stung eyes and summoned the haunting essence of her song. He moved with the visions she had forced into his mind. His leaden feet pulled free from their tenuous mooring and inched forward into the Circle.

At once, images and sounds enveloped him. He was walking through a glowing, dream-like forest in slow hypnotic steps. He perceived everything in radiant super-sense detail. The light, blunted by trees, was gently departing.

A group of women appeared through the trees, dancing around him. Their limbs were powerful, lithe and perfect as if fashioned by magic. He could smell a rich febrile odour from their skin. Trails of silver-blue hair fell from their heads, blazing like comet's tails. The women sang as they danced, their voices raw and enticing. The sound mesmerised him and conjured strange yearnings in his mind.

The song swirled in an endless round, each time gathering strength. It was music to grow lost in, and their fiery, galvanised faces glistened like polished amber, as their dance grew frantic.

Suddenly, one of the women leapt towards Dreamweaver. She tore off the strip of cloth that covered her sex and stood bare. Her face was wild, feline with delicate spirals gauged in the flesh. She held out her left hand, and in it, appeared, a jet-black dagger, whose fine-honed edge glimmered like dark and gaugeless crystal. She lifted the dagger above her head and began to dance.

She moved smoothly, the dagger carving circles in the air. Then she shook with wild, chaotic movements. Suddenly she stopped. Then, using both hands she guided the dagger to her belly and sank it deep into her flesh. There was a great cry from the women, and the song swirled like a serpent; it teamed with exotic darkness.

Dreamweaver gasped at the vividness, such raw uncensored perfection. She stared straight into his eyes, her gaze like beams of moonlight.

In time to the singing, she cut away great swathes of flesh, which instantly became a gleaming, transcendental substance. But her skin remained whole, clear and smooth. Without hesitation, Dreamweaver understood she was a magical form of existence. Free of time. Free of death. The woman whirled round and suddenly threw her dagger into the gloaming sky. The song spun like a fiery wheel as all eyes lifted to the dagger. It glided across the ghostly sickle of a new moon and a scream rose from the singers.

And then mixed with this came a sound like crashing thunder and the women vanished befor Dreamweaver's eyes. Their image flashed across his insight like a psychic shock-wave. He was shaking, his head throbbed and breath hissed in his throat.

In the space where the women had danced there now stood a thin, gaunt man, dressed entirely in figure-hugging black. He had a spiteful, once-handsome face, riddled with deep, emotional scars. His being was sullen with unwanted dangers and to look into his eyes could ruin you in an instant. He carried the malign energy of someone who had delved into the hidden depths of something wondrous, and discovered only fear and obscenity.

He began to walk towards Dreamweaver. 'Fool!' He snapped. 'Go back fool! Go back to your stories and lovers… LEAVE THIS CIRCLE!'

'Enough!' shouted Dreamweaver.

Somehow this presence seemed separate from the forest, like an angry spirit trapped between heaven and earth. His voice was sharp and crystallised with doom…

Dreamweaver roared, hurling the sound at the sinister figure, but he also vanished into nothing.

There was more still. New mysteries poured forth.

Once again Dreamweaver cried out for it to stop, but the Circle's elusive power-source was relentless. The forest crashed around him like a shattered mirror, revealing a new enchantment of pure white space. The powers of the Universe before the dark, the powers of the nameless, of madness... From unseen horizons came the lifeless hum of a vast hollowness, and he was momentarily seized by panic: to wander forever lost in eternal nothingness, he thought.

But before his mind could conjure more torment, he heard voices chanting in rhythms alien to him. His thoughts spun in their sound, morphing the words into the image of a male youth.

Wild hair the colour of fresh drawn blood swayed across a fast, deadly and almost feminine face. The youth's appearance, so strange, a being of intricate movement, a fiction of make-believe flesh. He moved across the void like speeding thoughts, clipped and smooth.

Others followed – male and female - washed in the same data.

Dreamweaver watched as they ingested what looked like strings of pure light. It slinked and twisted into their open mouths. They gasped as their bodies were surrounded instantly by a timeless, glacier-like stillness. He immediately perceived the strings as a portal to some unimaginable dream-realm.

Suddenly, he was inside their dream-sheath, floating alongside the youths. They moved above strange, dreaming cities, opaque as mosquito nets. Zooming down he saw they were crammed with the same mysterious beings. Somehow, he looked through their eyes and listened to their marix of psychic energy. He was filled with desire and wonder. His heart pounded deep in his chest; breath surged in and out…in…out, icing the lubrications of his tongue and mouth. Rivulets of sweat sleeked his face and flowed down his neck in a barbed necklace of crystal. He was at once amazed, confused, frightened and enchanted.

Finally, the intricate pattern of the circle wiped these images away. For an instant, the Circle blazed like a great star with a fiery corona. A heartbeat later, the Circle vanished, space imploded back into emptiness. Then came silence and with it darkness. Thick, meaningless darkness.

He fell to his knees exhausted. *I'm dead and living it*, he thought.

I'm dead.

Surely I am dead…

4

silence… silence… silence…

From within the vast no-thing, a sensation of stroking travelled up his spine.

His senses came alive as he leapt to his feet at lightning speed, arms outstretched.

Instantly the darkness shone like light, and he was facing a tall, slender woman dressed in skin-tight, auroral purple. The colour lived – flowed like liquid. His eyes fixed on her wild, idolatrous face, drinking her, feeling her with his mind. Instantly he knew her, yet she was infinitely strange.

Powerfully rendered features lurked behind thick, platinum hair, which fell gleaming to the floor. It was a face of destiny, worn like a sacred scar, and for an instant her entire body seemed timeless, unfettered by the transport of matter.

'You show me your face...' whispered Dreamweaver. But the words fell uncertainly from his lips.

Her eyes stared into his soul - Unblinking – shimmering like perpendicular halos. He felt they'd watched the beginning and ending of worlds upon worlds. They were glowingly present, yet filled with endless futures – aged, then young… aged… young.

A miraculous technology, he thought… an angel's transcendent flesh.

…Her mouth opened in a wave of gleaming slow-motion…

'It was no secret, Dream,weaver' she sang, 'and you have not searched for mere hunger's sake. I challenged you to find me, to look into my eyes and share my words, though at first you fought me with all your will.'

Her voice was benign and hypnotic, a prayer, a mantra, yet in the same instant, dangerous and sharp like daggers – a tongue to fashion pain.

Dreamweaver edged forward, eyes watchful, expectant. He reached out to touch her, but drew back. 'Who are you… what are you?'

…Her words now flowed in tiny movements... 'My name is Talis. The energy of this Sacred Circle has followed your Dream-Journeys, sensed your burning desire for change. The energy has now revealed the entrace to its hidden pathway.' She paused. 'I am woven into that pathway.'

Dreamweaver held his gaze firmly on her face. 'Then this is still a form of Dream-Journey, the work of Dream-Shamans.'

'It is easy to become confused,' replied Talis calmly. 'I am also part of the great power by which everything exists. I am light and time in this moment, as you are. But we are also thoughts that can travel beyond light and time.' She looked at him, eyes sparkling, then she laughed...

'Ultimately you must decide if I am real. But let us play with an idea. Has it crossed your mind that maybe it is I who is creating you. The real Dreamweaver lies rotting in the parched scrub clutching at spirits:::But think again:::Does that make this version of you less real:::?'

Before he realised, she reached forward and ran a long, pointed fingernail across his forearm.

He flinched. 'What the hell…'

A sharp pain gripped his arm. Her eyes flashed like diamonds. A thread of blood trickled and grew into a gushing stream of crimson. He put his hand in the stream, feeling it wet, warm and corpuscular. But he was shocked to find no wound.

'Real pain, or dream pain?' She asked. 'My pain or your pain? We are all in the business of creating.' Then with a simple mudra-like gesture she imploded the blood back into nothing.

Her words projected on his mind's eye. At first they were almost too rapid to recognise. Flashes. Spasms... almost thoughts. Then, a smooth, compelling clarity solidified.

He felt his angular face break into a smile. Why was he smiling?

She laughed in response, and the sound seemed luminous – hypnotic. 'And what would you have me do next?' She asked.

He studied her like a scripture. 'Many claimed that my mind was lost when I refused to continue my work as a Storyteller. They said that my stories had become a poison, and for a time I became confused; I even believed they were right.' He brushed a hand across his eyes as if to clean away the memory. 'But in this instant, I know that I exist through my own volition, and you are no figment. My uncertainty lies in how we can stand together in this place and be outside of a dream, in this Circle; a Storyteller and a Magical Interface.'

'Good, the faculty of choice is still strong within you, Dreamweaver. Storytelling has served you well,' she said.

'Let's see how well it serves,' Dreamweaver responded. 'To create intrigue, a Storyteller may compose this scenario. My mind has been invaded by a powerful, malignant force, which takes the form of a sensuous, miracle-clad woman.' His eyes fixed on her. 'This force will, of course, entice me with pleasures of the flesh, offer me many powers.' He paused for effect. 'In return for the energy of my soul.'

'You have tasted a new way of telling, seen your words create a power which extends beyond you. Words that summon anything into being by speaking its primal name. That is the great mastery you desire, the Dream-Shamans' energy eclipsed. Yet not for mere hungers sake. You imagine filling your world with such complex wonder.'

Dreamweaver looked at her. She was deep enough to drown in. His thoughts stirred like leaves in the wind, sending a shiver through his body. His breath coursed deep in his chest.

'Maybe my soul is the price you will demand. I have offered myself to strangeness and doubt without hesitation. Did I think that what lies in this Circle would cost me nothing?'

She looked deep into him. 'This was always your path. No matter what happens, this was always your path.'

Always..

Always…

5

A swathe of creating fog...

They walked out of the darkness into a counterfeit world...

A narrow path threaded through a landscape that grew knotted and wild. Dissolute sounds filtered through swaying, rhenium-leafed trees, faint pulses escaping from a hidden realm. A sharp, silver light bathed the scene, turning dust into splinters of diamond.

Dreamweaver's eyes picked out his reflection multiplied thousands of times in tiny, crystalline prisms of moisture strewn across the pathway. It seemed that every detail conspired to produce the impression that this was real. Plump fish splashed in small undulating streams, gleaming like polished metal. Emerald grass slicked with velvet lustre grew in thick insolent clumps, and cocoons dangled from gossamer-fine threads patiently awaiting their fictional future. Even a slight wind blunted by the abundance of fauna carried a frenzy of colourful, button-eyed insects to unplanned destinations, and scattered ingenious rotor-blade seeds from some life thirsty shrub.

Talis stopped and glanced at him. Then she moved off the path towards a clearing.

She turned and gestured. He followed her into a soft, shallow dip.

It was like the lap of a giant seated woman whose arms rested either side of her massive knees. Inside the dip, nothing showed past its edge except wild, untamed sky and the swaying canopies of heaven-bound trees. At the very centre the moist soil spawned a small shrine-like construction hewn from glass or crystal. It spread outwards, the length of a stride like a pigmy citadel. It sprouted tiny opalescent towers capped with sweet smelling sounds.

She leaned forward and gently plucked one of the miniature towers. Then handing it to him, she gestured.

'Lay down. Place it against your skin. Let it rest you,' she said. 'You've been on a long journey and you're still fresh to all of this. You will feel strange for a while. Rest first, then we will talk more.'

Tentatively, Dreamweaver lay down, suddenly tired and gripped by hunger. He was reluctant to give way to sleep, but gently held the miniature tower to his chest.

He began to feel an exquisite stillness and a sense of arousal came and went. His eyes followed streaks of crimson clouds as they kindled stars from their distant exile. He closed his eyes, drifted away.

Talis plucked another tower in a glistening wave of slow motion and fixed a place to sit. She spun the tower through her fingers, carefully propping her foot against a small rock.

>>>>>>>>>>>>>>

Dreamweaver awoke to the sound of Talis' song. He felt refreshed and invigorated, his hunger had vanished as if he had eaten a nourishing meal and drank from the purest spring.

She sat beside him.

He saw an overwhelming vastness in her ghost-kissed eyes. A gigantic wave of emptiness frozen before him, an invisible wall of consciousness. He remembered the women dancing in the Circle, and now saw Talis moving in time to their rhythm, her hair brushing their fervent limbs, her lips drawling with silver light.

'So now we begin,' he said, shaking the thought from his mind.

Talis smiled. 'Now we begin:::'

Talis stood up and placed her little tower back in the shrine. The way her body moved was extraordinary. Her flesh moved – one foot and then another – but her image seemed to come from elsewhere.

'What shall I do with the crystal?' asked Dreamweaver.

'Remember where it came from.' She stared into his eyes. 'I'm serious. Remember it.' With that she leaned over and snapped a tiny piece off the end. 'Open your mouth,' she insisted.

'My mouth?'

'It is natural for men not to trust, but you must overcome this reaction. Now open your mouth, or would you prefer I leave you to find your own way?'

He cautiously opened his mouth. She took the fleck of crystal and placed it against one of his back teeth. A searing flash of pain shot through his head. Instantly, he tried to grab her wrist, but his arm moved in ultra slow motion. Up it went... slow... slow... slow...

'There,' she said, withdrawing the fleck, 'teeth are the most crystalline structure in the human body. They are perfect for storing information.'

Shaken, he looked at her coldly. 'What information?'

'All will become clear when the time is right,' she replied.

Dispite his growing frustration, Dreamweaver felt compelled to look into her eyes. Part of him longed to be back on his journey to the Circle. He moved across his journey with pierced, zoom-filled vision, trained inwards to savour every moment, every pain, breath by breath. He contemplated his presence in this greater drama.

'You are afraid,' she said softly.

'No,' he replied, 'not anymore. If you fear what you seek, then you'll never arrive… I've come a long way to find an answer… a long way.'

Talis laughed gently; it sounded endless and intoxicating. 'Then I shall start…'

'When you entered the Circle, you gazed upon scenes lost to the Earth's memory, scenes from a time of wonderment and miracle. A time when dreams and imagination lived in all minds.' She stared into his eyes. 'But this was also a time of immeasurable tragedy, desire...and pain. Your eyes moved through this drama without understanding, like a language that cannot be spoken. However, just the sight of these alien shores has given you some preparation for what is about to happen. And my constant presence in your dreams ensured you came to this Circle with a mind crawling with desire...'

Her star-frosted features poured from the words.

'The Dreamweaver has called upon truth and it has answered, she said forcefully. 'You have been chosen to deliver a powerful resonance into your world. Through your lips the Story hidden in this Circle will again taste life, blood and breath. From your lips it will shape itself into a legend – you will speak it – speak it in the magical tongue. Those who take healing from your words will let it seep into their hearts and spread it to their children. They will remember the truth that has been hidden, and the power of dreams will once more stir within their minds.'

'Why don't you deliver this Story, this truth?' asked Dreamweaver. Then added: 'they will see you as a real Avatar, not a mere Storyteller that they have become comfortable with.'

She laughed. 'The realm of atoms has no blueprint to sustain my being. Besides, the Story I give you knows its own mind. It has waited patiently for you to arrive.'

'What if I refuse?'

A light shone inside her face. With a child's enthusiasm, she leant forward, her slender hands sliding back through her weightless hair. 'We will wait for the next one, and you'll go back to your stories knowing that the Earth carries more mystery than you imagined. Then, one day when your breath is weak, and the fire in your eyes has shrunk to a singe, you'll think this was a dream and smile:::then you'll begin to wonder...Oh, to have told the Story that changed everything.'

'Why do I still think I'm dreaming this?'

She looked up. 'This was always your path, Deken Nos-Antimon, you'll never walk away without knowing why the power of dreams, the power to cross the threshold of trance was lost. Storytellers are Mother Nature's desperate response to this blight, a slow and arduous road to restore her damaged children, to reconnect them to the thread of wonder. But you can bring them back in a stroke, Dreamweaver. You will never walk away without the sounds in this Story restoring your passion…I can give you them.'

'Enough!' Shouted Dreamweaver. 'You know something of me then. But tell me something in your words, let me feel their touch. what do you experience, what do you think you are?'

She looked thoughtful. Then sang her words. 'By some strange fate I find myself *in* the story and *of* it,' she sang. 'I'm the interface and the source:::an intricate transducer of mystery into form.'

She hesitated. 'I remember some things before this though….. I remember that something like me once experienced pain, and bled and felt the pounding of a beating heart. But these memories have become like inverted dreams, on waking I am clad in magical flesh. And the dream… the dream is where form stays fixed. I can never stop thinking in breathtaking sequence; I can never obliterate myself…' She stopped. 'I'm many things I don't yet understand.'

'Then we both have something to learn,' he said.

She laughed. 'It would seem so.'

In the sharpness of the moment, he edged himself forward. Then he made a movement to clasp her hand and she didn't draw back; it was warm and vivid and crawling with life.

'How real is real?' she asked. 'I'm no spectre pulled from the wilderness.' She smiled. 'Maybe I'm a demon plotting to deliver some terrible force into the world through your lips.'

'You see how my mind is working.'

She looked impossibly kinetic, alchemised from pure movement.

'There are miracles moving, travelling towards you, Dreamweaver. I see your mind is set on this journey. As we go deeper into the story, we'll be moving to stranger and more distant places, realms of immeasurable chaos. It's important to know that in these places I cannot guide you. You must find your own methods to gather the Story.'

'This is beginning to sound like a dangerous place.'

'All things are manifest in stories,' she responded. 'But in this complexity there are really only two paths. The first is simple: run from the chaos and it will enshroud and consume you. The second is infinitely more difficult and demands insight and considerable skill::: Focus and learn to recognise who and what, in the midst of the chaos, is not chaos, then believe in this, make it vital and beautiful. This is the stillness. There will be times when I speak in movement or silence, implanting scenes, sounds – feelings. Master each technique, my Dreamweaver, for in these places the eye conjures things that mean other things. An exquisite body...the stench of decay - an eclipsing sun...the smile of a lusting foe. Remember this and the foreignness will not deceive you.'

'What if I cannot make sense of it?' He studied her eyes, wondering what they saw.

'That's why it is you in the Circle. Use your gift, Dreamweaver, use it.'

He weighed the answer. 'The gift is finally tested,' he said.

'Before I describe my part in this drama, my purpose, so to speak,' she said. 'I will need to create a backdrop on which to begin your learning. For this, we travel back into a distant time on Earth, where a miraculous Sisterhood brought forth a technology which transformed living matter into a mystical spirit-like substance: an existence devoid of degeneration and death. The Sisterhood became known as the Sirens, sighting their abilities to entice and seduce through their strange beauty and voices.' She smiled. 'But that is only the tip, as you will see.'

'I've felt their presence,' said Dreamweaver. 'I've stood amongst these magical women undetected like a spirit.' Then added. 'Is that what you are, Talis, part of this Sisterhood, a Siren?'

Talis glanced away uneasily. 'You've seen something, but this is only a fraction of the picture.'

'You didn't answer my question.'

Anger flashed through Talis' eyes. 'Choose your path carefully, Storyteller and you will find understanding.' She paused, 'now let us continue.'

He remained unmoved, studying the sky. It was crystal blue splashed with vermilion streaks. Strange designs floated across the fugitive sun. A line of gleaming white clouds sitting below the streaks caught his attention as they aimlessly drifted. He felt a warming breeze, a delicate caress against his cheeks. The incense of imagination came on the breeze. Foreign tongues, ecstatic bodies, exotic pigments – swirling...

'After the Sirens appeared on Earth,' continued Talis, 'they self-fertilised, creating a race of immortal Warriors to act as consorts and guardians of their "Spirit Technology". Together they surrounded the Earth with an entirely new dimension devoid of time and entropy. This was known as THE SEED. But the power needed to create and sustain such a magical realm was vast beyond belief. With a flash of genius, the Sirens discovered what they needed. Encased in the human mind, between the synaptic leap, was the raw material of impossibility, the stuff that dreams are made from. Such a potent commodity could be used to sustain The Seed. However, they soon discovered that the power of dreams is useless without the rich fuel of...'

'Imagination,' interrupted Dreamweaver. '...Imagination...'

His face turned pale and drawn.

Talis looked into his eyes. 'So humanity struck its most dangerous deal. In return for human Dream-Power and Imagination, those with power were granted the perogative of the Gods. They were given the chance to journey into a sparkling realm of never-ending stimulation. The Seed was a chance to escape the clutches of age and death, a chance to transcend the limits of Earthly Creation.'

She gently touched Dreamweaver's hand, sending a surge of energy through him. 'So many disagreed, they tried everything in their power to stop it, but the leaders of your world silenced them. The rich and powerful did their bidding beyond the reach of ordinary people, and soon even the most skillful dissenters fell silent. Consequently, the Sirens delved into Dream-Power using their miraculous technologies and uncovered the source of human imagination. They began harvesting this treasure.'

Her grip tightened around his fingers. 'Most of your human history has been spent trying to escape the eroding curse of time in one way or another. Oh, to take such an opportunity. What harm could come from sharing something that science said was never-ending, infinite? Can you honestly say you would not take such a chance?'

Dreamweaver shook his head. 'So I am to beleive that the Sirens took our greatest gift.'

Talis laughed hauntingly.

Dreamweaver snatched his hand away in anger.

'Steady yourself,' insisted Talis. 'The story will reveal a truth very different from what you are expecting. Do you really think it could be that simple? For now, it is enough to say that the Sirens were a facet, but not the mechanism that caused the Great Loss. This must be clear in your telling of the story.'

'How can such an episode be hidden from our memory, why do the Storytellers not pick it up from their travels in the dream-realm?'

'You Storytellers cannot see what has passed through the minds of your ancestors. Only through me have you laid eyes on such things. You walk through fresh dream pastures; the quantum newly births your gift and the wonder of the places it takes you. Only by releasing this story from the Circle will this truth and what was lost be set free. Your time will unite once again with his-story, her-story. All dream realms will merge and once again become one, and the process of healing will take place. Through you, the work of the Storytellers will be complete, the world will run thick with your words and the freedom of creation.'

Deken Nos-Antimon, the weaver of dreams, shook his head. 'How can this be?'

Talis reached over and lifted his chin so that their eyes met.

'Slowly... We're jumping too far ahead. I won't let you down, I am here to help you make that leap of faith, quench your terrible thirst. But you must unfold the story in its full glory. And thus we must begin with the Sirens. We must trace their origin, understand how they came to possess such awe-inspiring abilities. For this we must leave Earth far behind and go back yet further in time to a distant planet called Teloset... back... back.... back we go...'

6

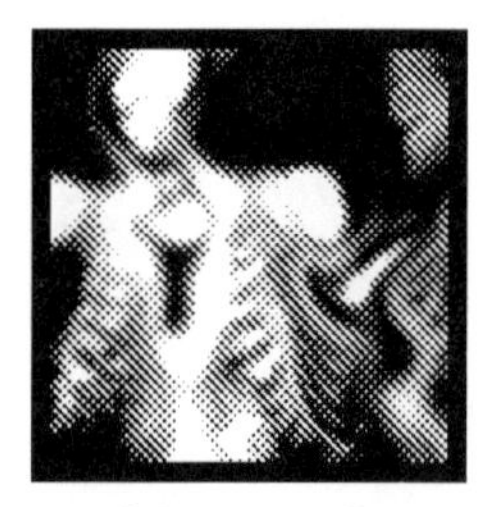

swirls of sentient static.......

Evocative sensations scrawled through Dreamweaver's body, but images lurked nervously at the edges of his awareness. He found this disconcerting but magnetic, like balancing on the edge of a precipice, or touching an unknown lover in a darkened room.

He sensed other experiences as though he was dreaming – conscious that he was dreaming – able to distinguish forms as they changed. This dream-state imbued him with senses, which he knew he couldn't possess.

Yet he did...

Talis' voice drifted like static beamed from a distant galaxy. 'Fix yourself, Dreamweaver::::::fix yourself.'

Thoughts with fuzzy edges blossomed into visuals, and his eyes slowly adjusted. He stared in disbelief as a shiver ran up his spine. Uneasiness gripped him. He opened his mouth to speak, but only silent breath left his lips.

Words fell backwards into his mind...

He found himself standing inside a structure so psychically extrovert that it practically declared itself impossible.

Giant pillars of crystal-clear flames blazed heavenwards, piercing a vast, spectral dome, filled with blinding light like a dazzling garment of chastity. The light was impregnated with exquisitely complex patterns, which moved in smooth logic-distorting sequences.

A brilliantly illuminated altar stood at the far end of the edifice emblazoned with mythologies.

With incredible force, a crowd surged into the temple from all sides, bodies adorned with dancing gases, garments of ectoplasm. Small ghostly creatures with soft, angelic faces pierced the enamelled flesh of the women's breasts like tamed incubuses.

The men bled geometric chants from deep facial scars.

A feminine chorus began singing from within the crystal flames; atoms filled with magic.

Dreamweaver swung his gaze moving with the crowd, felt his own breath catch in unison with those around him. Snatches of foreign tongues brushed his ears, sounding like raspy whispers. He sensed the element of himself, which was one with all those around him, but the differences formed a deadly contradiction.

They can't see me... They can't see me...

He stared across the throng towards the altar. A profound hush spread through the temple, followed by a great moan that swept like a wave through the crush of bodies. It was vital and beautiful. He exhaled with the enraptured presence that surrounded him.

The crowd gazed up in unison; he followed their gaze.

A cluster of amazing women emerged from the shimmering dome above; their creamy tanned bodies sparkled like polished gems. They floated down towards the altar as though they were weightless wisps, and the crowd gasped in awe as their luminous feet touched the floor.

At once he recognised an image so familiar to his being that it froze his eyes. His senses remembered them with breath-stilling shock. The trails of silver-blue hair, the perfect limbs, and the smell that belched from their alien flesh. The Goddess gaze charged with tyrannous force. Now their roots were exposed to him; a vision-echo come full circle.

Their voices caressed his mind. Living sound. Hypnotic. Musical:

'The sun that burns in the sky ~ gives life by the force of a lie,'
they sang.
'The earth that falls at your heels ~ can never be what it feels,'
the chorus sang.
'The child that lies in your arms ~ is timeless and laden with charms,'
the women cried.
'The girl with eyes made of fire ~ will weave you the flesh of desire,'
the chorus sang.
'The man with hands made of light ~ will take you away in the night,'
the women sang, their hair flowing like water in space.

Somehow he understood their words as they streamed forth. He felt infested with time, every cell exposed to a bastard-reality concealed from the sight of nature. His mind eavesdropped on eternity and sensed the touch of a fugitive atom.

He watched transfixed as the tallest and most astonishing of all the Goddess creatures moved to the centre. Then, placing a hand inside her belly she drew out a sphere of gleaming flesh from deep within. It pulsed like mercury come alive.

The crowd screamed with delight, tears streamed, as she raised it above her head.

Silence fell.

Then she spoke in a voice so clear and truthful that Dreamweaver found himself overcome with emotion.

'My people,' she said slowly. 'It is time to set this great gift free into the Universe, may it seek out all those in need of its power and healing. May it journey to the stars. My immortal essence is contained within this vessel. My body will tread the soil of other worlds and fulfil my purpose, the purpose of the Great Creator. And when each mission is complete, the embodiment of my soul will re-enact this sacrament on their alien world. In this way my gift will propagate the Universe with light. May it go with love.'

The Sphere began to float up from her hands...

Dreamweaver stood mesmerised, staring at her.

Without warning, a great sorrowful moan came from behind; followed by screams of terror. A huge wind raged through the temple, tightening around the crowds. All eyes swept around and stared in horror at a creature making its way towards the Goddess. It howled, and its mouth gaped open in a great festering wound. The stench was unbearable.

As it walked, clouds of rotting flesh flew from its body like acid confetti, scorching people's faces and bodies. At first glance, only imagination could place it in the human realm, yet in a sense there was something womanly beneath its ugly symmetry.

The Goddess made no attempt to avoid the loathsome creature, her face remained still, calm, unmoved. And then, it stood before her. Time froze. Breath stopped. The floating Sphere ceased its ascension.

The Repugnance broke the glacier stillness.

'Look at what your gift creates,' it said in a pestilent voice.

The Goddess looked at it with her sparkling eyes. 'You have only to act for it to be different,' she said softly. 'You have created what stands before me through your actions.'

The Repugnance flicked her gaze at the floating Sphere, and for the first time the Goddess faltered.

Quicker than thought, the Repugnance leapt for the sphere and caught it. It hissed with displeasure, and clouded with smears.

The Goddess screamed out. 'NO!' And a great wail of sorrow rose from the crowd. She reached out to send her energy into the sphere, but it now screamed like a banshee.

The other Goddesses moved forward, but she held out her hand to stop them. 'Wait,' she ordered, 'we cannot risk the Vessel, we must be gentle.'

Something vaguely resembling a smile washed across the Repugnance's face.

'You take my dream, I take your dream,' she spat.

'You can still experience the touch of salvation.' said the Goddess. 'It doesn't have to end this way.'

'Oh yes it does,' said the Repugnance, 'I'm so sick of all this living.' She laughed, sending a ribbon of mucus across the beautiful face of the Goddess. 'And don't try your magical chants with me, will you. You see, it won't work because I don't care about anything any more. My force now lives inside your 'blessed' creation, so I no longer have any use for this miserable existence.'

Suddenly, in one shocking action, she drove her fingers through the putrid flesh of her chest, and tore out her heart. She held it up in her skeletal fingers, pulsating and luscious. 'There,' she said, 'here we have it.'

For what seemed like an eternity, she looked deep into the gleaming eyes of the Goddess, and for a second she hesitated. 'I....... I.... Lov... y... o' she seemed to stammer, then gave up.

Like a thrusting rapier all of the goddesses flew at her, eyes blazing. But the Repugnance made no attempt to evade them, simply closing her fingers around the heart.

It stopped beating.

A blinding flash. Searing heat. Vaporised flesh.

In that last instant, a sequence flashed across Dreamweaver's mind:

The blemished Sphere rocketing out through the dome, hurtling into the heavens...

He seemed to see it moving through space like a dark comet. He could hear the terrifying laugh of the Repugnance echoing through the Universe.....

(((Talis was dark static, a jet statue against a night sky)))

'Welcome back,' she said, her voice like a soft brush drawn across metal.

Dreamweaver stared in silence.

'Very, disturbing,' she said. 'But this little segue is only the beginning. We need to journey back yet further to take us to this flash-point.'

She smiled, then suddenly looked very serious. 'Mark carefully what you've just seen,' she said. 'As you will discover, it is the absolute fulcrum of the whole story, the core. If you lose your way, return to it.'

She looked deep into his eyes. 'Clear?'

'Clear,' whispered Dreamweaver, then added. 'Is that where you're from, Talis?... Yes... I can see they were your Sisters.'

Her eyes flashed.

'We will come to that later,' she said coldly. 'Now for you to be able to transmit the Story, leaving no gaps, no holes, we need to place some meaning and context on the events you've just seen. This requires us to visit and understand the ancient myths of their soil, travelling deeper still into the womb of time.'

Dreamweaver looked down. 'Maybe I am scared after all. I feel like a ghost trapped inside a dream, searching for evidence that I once lived and told stories to people.'

She glared at him.

'I've warned you to be careful how you work this,' she growled. 'And now you know how it can pull you off if I am not there to bring you back. It will get even more complex though. As a Storyteller, you don't need me to tell you that ghosts can be more real than the flesh they discarded. They can love, they can destroy. They have no need to know of their own existence; their effect on the Universe can be seen, yet they're nowhere to be found. Dreams carry the same indent. Nations rise and fall in them, lovers are exalted and destroyed: all by the power of dreams. But where are they when a spurned lover swallows the pills? Gone...gone without trace.'

She stayed silent for a long time, then said, 'don't concern yourself with too many definitions, Dreamweaver, real...dream...ghost, it's all the same. This story is fickle like fate; study what you fix upon, bathe in it if you like, but don't think these are your thoughts. The more you feel like you belong, the less you must belong.'

Dreamweaver studied her face. He remembered the first time she had appeared in his Dream-Journey. The way she had enticed him without ever exposing her face; the heightened state he'd experienced. Now, of course, he knew feelings of greater strength. He'd moved in them and breathed the scent of Methuselahs. His flesh crawled with exotic impressions.

'Chaos sifted into order,' he said. 'Control and abandon made one.'

'Do not become lost in ideas,' she said dryly, 'there's still a vast distance to journey.'

'I'm listening,' he responded

Talis smiled, looking at the sky as though trying to probe into a realm beyond.

'We reverse the coarse mixture of time,' she said presently.

7

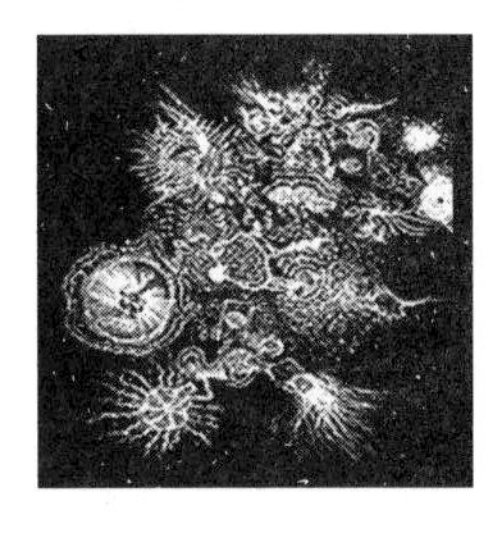

'Such a lush cache of myths enveloped the reign of Namida, the Teloset Empress,' explained Talis. 'It's difficult to see the markings of sentience behind those veils, yet to learn this facet of our story, it is necessary to place her within the boundaries of human intelligence. To verify the force set in motion through her dark and sectarian mind, you must call upon your own concept of malignance.'

'What does Namida mean?' Asked Dreamweaver.

'All Teloset languages are incomprehensible to human ears. The word Namida is the closest your tongue can get to the original vernacular. The meaning we can attribute to it, is purity or unspoilt.'

'I can already sense the irony.'

'Believe it,' said Talis. 'Namida was the daughter of a powerful demagogue. When her father died under mysterious circumstances, she quickly assumed power with the backing of his grief-stricken army.'

'So far away in time and distance, yet the patterns of power and intrigue remain the same,' he observed.

She smiled a half-second smile then said: 'This alone would make a fascinating tale, but our task is not to look at what can readily be seen, but to find different perspectives. Every leap of a synapse, every word spoken, love-making, anger, slaughter... These are the surface patterns, yet what meanings lie beyond them?'

He nodded.

'Within a short time,' continued Talis. 'Namida's unremitting violence brought all but a fraction of Teloset under her control. The lips of dissenters were welded shut by the threat of her vehement and sadistic acolytes. She was loathed and exalted with equal vigour. Stories abounded of her dark psychic prowess. Word spread that she was an adept, schooled in the evil practice of Womb-Trancing – plundering the abundant energy of newly conceived life as it sits in its mother's belly.

'Sobbing and screams drifted through her palace like the pheromones of fear and sadness. And her extravagant beauty did much to swell such rumours; her skin was as smooth as silk and glowed as white as the finest milk. Her eyes sparkled with the purest green, like emeralds lit from within, her hair long and straight like a fall of black water. She was chasteless vice – blasphemous, terrifying and somehow inevitable.

'But despite her seemingly invincible power, this exquisite vestment of skin and veins hid a deep and twisted neurosis. At the merest hint of her increasing years, Namida would seethe with anger and tremble with fear, seeing that her beauty was as transient as all things cloaked in flesh, plate or shell. Dark eddies in her mind soon fixed on the moduless silence of death, and she banished the words time, age and death from every conceivable vernacular. Clocks ran backwards, nature was hidden from her sight, she slept in rooms bathed in ceaseless light, her eyes fixed open and staring. No day, no night. No elemental movement penetrated her taut retinas.

'When all this happened, how advanced was their understanding of reality?' asked Dreamweaver. 'Were there no mechanisms, no potions...?'

She shook her head, 'nothing that had any lasting effect,' she replied. 'Namida ordered the greatest minds to pierce the womb of providence to retrieve the transcendent gene. With the threat of hideous torture and the death of their families hanging over their heads, thousands of brilliant scientists enciphered their lives through this brawling contrivance. No civilisation had ever seen such a lavish assault on time and death. But despite this immense effort, the rampant emptiness of matter echoed with their failures.'

'No one tried to stop her?'

'The atmosphere ran thick with myth,' explained Talis. 'Even the most powerful dissenters smelt the scent of some prescient wonder. They too lived in the grip of their hungers. They shared her problem of mortality.'

'Yes, the desire to live and live,' he observed.

'A terrible sting bled from this. In the ensuing years, the language of entropy raged through her zealot flesh, carving with its sharpened tongue. Her once radiant eyes became hooded and filled with sadness, her voice roared like thunder, and it seemed all bitterness and anger had been sucked inside her. "Bring me more life," she screamed. A pungent hatred infested her eyes as she stared out of her gilded prison at the young and beautiful women attending to her orders. Her tears had long since dried, and her body was as dry as shell, a husk abandoned by joy.'

Talis was quiet for a long time.

'Loathing boiled in Namida's breast,' she said finally. 'She'd become a sampler of atrocities most couldn't even imagine. Driven almost insane by the presence of youth and beauty, she decreed that every young person under twenty years would be defaced until all trace of nature's radiance was erased. No longer would she gaze upon an unspoiled body. No longer would she sense the prodigy of smooth, untarnished flesh and…'

'Surely she came unravelled?'

Talis shook her head. 'No, this was not a place of courage and great luxurious thinking. Most misjudged Namida's power over symbol and mind, and the willingness of her conglomerate to action such an affront.'

She smiled, but her face was clouded with pain. 'There's never a shortage when the dark side of nature is armed with the force we call Law.'

'True, but I still can't see how a miracle such as Spirit Technology emerged from such a crude cultural mess? We've seen despots and tyrants on Earth – great towers of dead biology. We've seen the alchemist's vision surpassed by thinking machines… but never a leap of such magnitude.'

'Yes, of course,' she said. 'We all know destruction and chaos have circled around and around until we're sick. But the scenes we're studying now have played only once; the circle's never been joined. I don't know, maybe that is the point… I just don't…'

She stopped. 'I'm learning something too,' she said. 'I'm learning that the Story is not what I thought, and I begin to see that like the characters in a story, the self I project moves only through conflict.'

'Explain,' urged Dreamweaver.

'There's a new awareness in me, but I can't express it in words. A series of pictures gleaned from deep within the story. A string of images, almost too blurry to mean anything.'

He looked at her and smiled. 'Don't force it. The more you feel like you belong, the less you must belong.'

'All right,' She said smoothly. 'You're very quick….very smart.'

'Something's hiding beneath the surface of your story,' he said, laughing. 'I have travelled through enough dreams to know…All stories contain secrets hidden from their teller…'

Her eyes shone with a mischievous glint. 'We must move in close again and live the events,' she said quietly, 'grasp the mundane and the spectacular – bathe in the sentient stream.'

Dreamweaver looked intent. 'Please continue.'

'Now, as I'm sure you've guessed,' said Talis, 'Teloset was no ordinary planet. It was a vast goddess of dirt and crystal. Its equators were seeded with dark, dreaming deserts. Its forests brimmed with strange humanic plants capped with vaporous heads. And glowing zirconium ghizas spluttered over mountains and tundra teased by chattering winds. Such a setting naturally grew myths and superstitions.'

'And in Namida's time the people believed and feared these mystiques?'

'More than you can imagine,' she replied. 'Belief was still rampant in most minds - such things skilfully underpinned Namida's jihad. A sordid stream of charlatan prophets, sooths, shamans and counterfeit scriptures deemed her atrocities necessary to obtain the secrets of immortality. She played it like some vast overseer was working a great mechanism through her hand.'

'Again, the pattern.'

He drew his gaze away from her and looked up into the sky. How can I be here, he thought? How is this possible?

'Now we come to the twist,' explained Talis. 'Namida's sordid infliction had spread like a stench across Teloset. Many tribes abandoned their inner wisdom and delivered their young to the process, believing they'd be restored and given eternal youth when Namida pleasured death's zygote. Imagine a world where creatures just lived for pain, sang night and day of pain, of receiving it. There was no innocence to escape into.'

She leaned closer speaking almost in a whisper, 'but everything changed when Namida's sadistic troops ventured to the borders of a remote province, a province shrouded in an ancient myth. The land, which lay beyond the threshold of a corpse-flecked river, was a sickening, irascible waste, a dark and malignant void. Every crawling vestige of life was purged from its soil, and flesh became putrid at the merest stroke of its breeze.'

'And what about the myth?'

'Not what you might expect,' she said sharply. 'The facts are at my disposal, so I'll tell it in my own way.'

'Tell it how you wish.'

'...The myth told how countless years ago, on the flange of this sickened zone, the most beautiful daughter of a powerful Chief was betrothed to the murderous Prince of a neighbouring tribe. She detested the sight of this sordid beast, and vowed that the marriage would never take place.

'But much was at stake. Without this partnering her scheming father could look forward to years of disruption and threat. His daughter possessed a wild, eroticized beauty; dark flesh flowed like oil over fine, ripened bones. Thick phosphorescent hair plunged from her head in a single radiant helix and large feline eyes sparkled above slanted cheeks, whiteless and crammed with feelings. Her lips were sculpted and moist with untold lust.

'But like a midsummer lake there were things hidden below this perfect surface. She possessed a keeness of mind that belied her years, and strength of will more akin to a master. The greedy Chief saw the value of these gifts. Her allurement to all genders combined with intelligence would prove a powerful weapon of corruption. In his enemy's tribe she would be the flame of a candle dancing on its wick, consuming the wax beneath, as a virus tears body from soul. She understood her father's plan, but she couldn't accept such a miserable fate.

'Early one morning as ghostly x-ray mists swirled around her delicate ankles, she left her tribe and walked towards the River of Death. She knew of only one place that all tribesmen feared to enter. She moved quickly towards the river, past thousands of slaves chained along its vomit-soaked boundary. They watched mesmerised as she calmly waded across the River of Death and stood upon the opposite shore, radiant. The ground beneath her feet liquefied and came alive, yet she remained untouched by its poisonous elements.'

'So somehow this retched mire welcomed her – wanted her?' asked Dreamweaver.

'It did more than that,' explained Talis. 'The myth tells how it nurtured and cherished her, how it coated her flesh with a nitrous fog. It describes in detail how snake-like creatures, engorged with shimmering poisons, bubbled with pleasure about her legs.

'In our minds we watch these images…feel them… These creatures moved towards her sex in slow, reaching movements, and swathes of vapour explored her nostrils and mouth – the kiss of a nitrous shadow.

'She became absorbed in the bliss of a vision. "Yes," she screamed, "watch, watch me destroy this flesh, the flesh that my own father would give away, watch this flesh fall to the darkened soil. This poison land will be my only lover…"

'The slaves broke free from their chains, powered by a new strength, the land screamed with delight. She threw back and laughed. She pulsed, glinted and moved to invisible rhythms, locked in a strange slow dance. Great poems of fluid drained from her lips. Then, like the tearless cut of a keratin horn, her flesh fell away and she bled into trans-existence. Her tzelem, her soul was bathed in a new wave of matter, intelligence wrapped in a dream. She had no need of a heart, no need of blood; she needed only thought to summon a gleaming semblance.

'The slaves sang and danced on the river's edge. Sen, Sen Sen, they called, Sen the Goddess of Freedom, it went on and on, an orgy of sound and sweat. The place reeked of transcendental power; sentient beings had never before witnessed such a making.'

There was a pause.

Dreamweaver sat upright and still. He let a silence fall and didn't disturb it. A dizziness swirled his mind. Her words filled him with superabundance, a lexicon of new sensations. He thought again that perhaps he was dead, that this was some kind of mental facet of eternity. He felt a pain in his head, the pain of something living. He breathed…and breathed…

'You're alive,' she said in a soft voice.

He hesitated for a moment, then faced her with a question: 'And you, are you alive?'

She turned. 'I see that my existence is… I see something …'

'What is it, Talis? What do you see?' He demanded. 'Search for it…'

She smiled inwardly. 'I think sometimes, when I want to comfort myself, that I died long ago, and by some strange fate I'll never have to face oblivion. The concept of oblivion is so fixed upon earthly things is it not? And yet, this is the paradox: if I only exist in this story, outside of time, how can I still evolve? How can I still think of my dissolution?'

She sounded just a little scared, and she turned sharply and looked into Dreamweaver's eyes. 'Part of me remembers thinking of all the creatures forever frozen in the measureless stillness of death. I remember…' she stopped.

He nodded. 'What can it mean to escape death? The diminished world grasps at Storytellers for hope. We conjure worlds where the essence of men and women lives on; we tell how earthly bodies are only a stage …that we transcend. We stroke the fear of the masses. They see providence reflected in our eyes, our words seep like morphine into their minds and ease their pain. Yet who carries *our* fears? We are borne with senses that can only be understood by a few…'

'Fear hides in darkness,' she whispered. 'Your journey into darkness has been long and cruel. The goal you have now accepted is the goal of knowledge, and in your desire lies its accomplishment.'

'And what about you?' he asked. 'What is there for you?'

She thought a long time before answering. 'I only know I'm to give you this story. Sometimes I glimpse myself somewhere else … but I get in my own way. I cannot see through myself.'

He was gripped by her temporal image; her words touched him in waves of tempting acoustic. 'Your Story is complex, wild and beautiful,' he said. 'We must open it fully and find those glimpses.' He watched her accept this, then added carefully: 'now…we left the slaves dancing at the birth of a Goddess,'

'Yes,' she said. 'The myth continues. Men from the two tribes swept the land looking for the missing Princess, their faces daubed with crimson and leprous yellow. Warriors blackened like carbonised velvet spread out at the front, swords glistening and lurid. The girl's father marched at the centre of the throng, entombed in the heaving mass of bodies. Dark drooling caves of anger sucked the world into his mind and shaped it as sour and rapacious. Had she dared to disobey him? Had she eloped with a secret lover? Or had she been abducted by an enemy tribe? The fear of humiliation fueled his blistering rage. The throng moved in a sprawling dimension destroying anything in its path. The chief acted on instinct, guiding his men to the River of Death. All that mattered in the world: to search and find the Princess.

'The last sepia gloss of light burned on every blade and bead of sweat, on every withered leaf and stem, on the polished viscera of trampled insects. It burned in the air. Through this glimmer, great clouds laden with thunder drifted in to claim the day, vaporous citadels crammed with electrical souls. As they drew close to the river, the ways became narrower, filthier, the men clasped their faces to block the odours of entropy; each step delivered a greater assault. Then they saw the slaves' vanquished chains, the imprints of frenzied movement written in the mud. They saw skeletal beasts licking at blood-like clods, mouths slavering, eyes like burning gems, and they heard the thick, resinous water, keening its acrid sadness.

'The tingling afterglow of ecstatic abandon crawled on their skin, and they sensed the flash of a dreadful portent cloaked in its touch. Hands trembled and their teeth chattered with an icy expectance; something played with their naive psyches. The impenetrable formation of men became loose and agitated, blurred at the edges. "Forward, damn you!" cried the Chief. "We are men, not frightened boys!!" Then they saw the portent materialised in its full glory, and the chief's face galvanised with terror…

'The radiant semblance of Sen hovered above the opposite bank, an apparition, naked and glorious, her shimmering, spectral flesh casting an eerie lunar glow into the sunlit world. Thousands of fine, milky threads protruded from the area of her sex, spreading out in a giant, arachnid display: they extended some distance, gently moving as if they floated in some kind of invisible fluid. To fulfill the purpose of this astral mechanism, globules of frosted light at the end of each umbilical coagulated into perfect replicas of their hoste, until the sky ran thick like a great, sprawling aviary.

'The men were terrified as never before, but stayed transfixed by what towered over them. The warriors had frozen not more than ten paces from the water's edge, then parted like silk unfolding as the Chief moved forward. His imploded mouth gaped, framed by a thick, fear-bleached beard. He stood at the water's edge, shrunken and insignificant. "I am to mourn death and life in one act," he said in a faltering, bitter voice. "An evil contrivance made from a vessel of beauty."

'Sen stared down at the puny figure. "Father, go back, go back". Her soft, melodic voice seemed to echo from every direction. "Take your men and return home. There is no harm for you if you go in peace." The splay of umbilicals dropped from their moorings as she floated down. Her unbound anatomy seemed in a constant state of becoming, splitting and dividing, like a healing cancer, yet she was still a woman, carrying the resonance of everything feminine and animalistic. Now the soil had taught her more: she understood how moons make love to planets by stirring their seminal oceans, and how a million lifetimes are a single moment in the span of one love-making. Yes...she also understood the minds of men: Gods wrapped in reptile and ape.

'She hovered a hand's length from the earth, effortless and magnificent, and gazed at the scene before her. Very slowly and gently her duplicates fell earthward, forming long and sensual lines on each flank; and with this motion came a new spectacle. At first they were identical in every aspect, then each Avatar evoked a new and unique countenance – some lush and girl-like, some strong-featured and cleverly muscled, others more boyish and anabolic.

'The men gasped, a shudder moved through their ranks. Their stupefied faces stared in disbelief. Sen's gaze penetrated them; they couldn't avoid her invasion. "Go," she urged again. "I do not wish you to die like fools for nothing."

'The chief regained his cold self-possession. "Evil!" he bellowed, "we will destroy you all, destroy this curse."

'Sen spoke for the last time. She spoke past the Chief. "If there are any among you that are courageous enough to be themselves, turn away from this now." She gestured. "To be oneself is a precious thing, and a rare one. I have received a gift from this ancient and poisoned land. I have learned to move past death and to believe in it too, but not to rejoice over it, to indulge in it. I set before you no army, no curse, no nightmare. I set before you a miracle. As long as you hate, and burn with anger, there will be only limits to what you can do. You will be at the mercy of these things. Anger is a consuming force, and hatred is blinding; when men take action to discipline these forces great things are possible. Don't cripple yourselves any more. Choose the light of life...."

'The throng became agitated, and at last, a few of the assembly seemed to comprehend, and turned away. A heartbeat later the tribe's elite hacked them down. The echoes of the executioners' blows took longer to die than their victims, and with this last ignoble act the future arrived. Sen and her protean daughters began singing in unison – a whole universe of clashing, chromatic fields melded into a vast and sensual slab of sound that pierced the minds of the onslaught.

'This action was enough to push men beyond the limits of self-control. With a high pitched cry they surged forward. Their future clogged with hormones, insanity coursed through their eyes, and lust seeped from their loins to fuel their purpose. Hysteria instantly ignited, spilling them down into the acrid torrent.

'In the mind-shattering frenzy a half-skinned foot trampled the chief's foaming skull, flesh steamed, men screamed, eyes belched fire, hands groped here and there, reaching for lost salvation. Bodies floated face down, their rot wasted on the lifeless spume. Severed limbs sank into the mud like some unnameable species. At last the River drank them all and covered each corpse with its rippling sheet. Sen removed her voice from the Sirens' choir and silence fell across the land. The world was grey and blue, metallic and growing dim… They turned and disappeared into the mist.'

Talis leaned back.

It was almost daylight.

She touched his eyes. 'Rest now or you'll grow weak, your memory will fade.'

'Clever,' he said. 'The story unfolds… yes it unfolds. I can connect one thing to another,' he hesitated, 'the Sirens exhumed from a myth. The next piece is how this force transformed into the evil of Namida, and then…and then…how it journeyed to Earth. Past and future synchronous…past and future…'

'That I'll tell you when you awake. I'll tell you everything.'

'Gone,' he said. 'I'm dreaming – this is a dream. You cannot exist.'

'Gone…' she whispered. 'Gone, my Dreamweaver.'

8

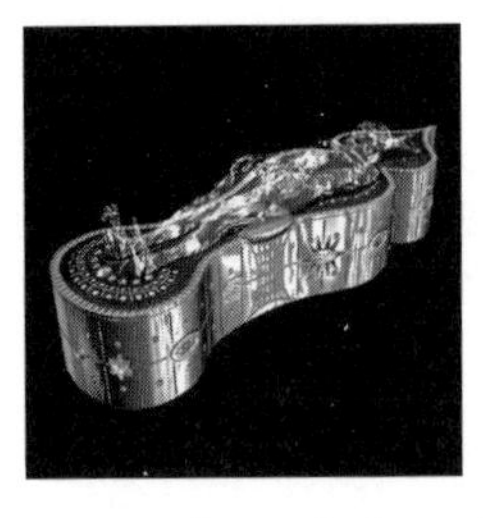

Dreamweaver awoke with a start. He felt cold and hungry. It was dark. Shadows moved within him instead of thoughts, and strange odours assaulted his nostrils. The air he drew into his lungs carried this stench deep inside him. He leapt to his feet. Twisted in darkness. He felt suddenly that he existed in some other mind, and that he might become lost in its convolutions.

'Talis,' he called. 'Talis, what is this?' His voice echoed as if he was encased in some kind of chamber.

His eyes peered into the gloom, and now perceived a mistiness moving towards him. He felt himself grow aware of this place and sensed a terrible danger. Then, striding out of the mist there came something shaped like a man, it flew at him screaming like a banshee, fastening onto his neck, weaving its fingers into his flesh. A shimmering light rose between them like smoke, revealing part of a face: crazed eyes seared into his skull like burning napalm, driving a jagged fissure through his mind. He stared into their fire, and for a moment he felt consciousness slipping away. He struggled to stay. His breath burst from him as he was thrown back against something solid. Next he landed a mighty blow into a pulsing chest, but it took the hurt in its stride. Suddenly, the smeared features seemed to crystallise into one coherent form, his assailant revealed. This was no malformed demon, no force conjured from darkness. This was the face of a man like him, a face he knew; a face lodged deep in his psyche.

With this he summoned new strength and threw him off. The fighting power was mustering in his hands. Again the figure attacked. Dreamweaver parried and turned to meet the assailant in open combat.

The figure seemed drawn like a magnet to his throat, but this time he offered only confusion; he was an anti-target, fists becoming blurs amongst blurs, throttling until the figure started to lose its human shape.

In the recess of his mind there grew a sense of self-control, then stillness. His heart pounded almost out of his chest. The air smelt sharp and caustic. The attacker slumped to the floor in a crumpled heap.

He lowered his gaze to fix upon the face of the man that had warned him away from the Circle. The unforgettable once handsome face wracked with obscenity, the hate-flecked eyes, and the figure-hugging black ~ all there in vivid holographic detail, a synaptic flash, a vision come alive, made real enough to kill.

The crumpled heap spoke. 'Fool!' He snapped. 'I warned you to go back, you had only to turn your mind, now you must die…'

'Who are you?'

'I'm something that was Peter Lynium,' the figure hissed.

'Peter Lynium,' repeated Dreamweaver. 'It means nothing to me.'

'That makes no difference,' Lynium snapped. 'And if I'd had my way it never would.'

Dreamweaver considered this exchange, remaining alert. 'You said I had only to turn my mind, but now I must die. What do you mean?'

A wry smile broke across Lynium's tarnished features. 'You think you're learning a story, a lost onomatopoeic that will satify your craving and bring healing to your damaged world…well you're wrong, so wrong,' he gasped. 'It will only bring more misery. You suspected it yourself...but ignored your instincts and my warning.'

His image seemed to be fading, and his voice came from a greater distance. 'Talis fooled you, she lied to you. When you first stepped into the Circle, you had merely to shift your focus to return to the world. But now, you have two miserable choices: to reach the end of the Story and spread its contagion, or die in this counterfeit reality: die with all the pain that stories can conjure.'

Dreamweaver considered the statement 'What if I never tell the Story?'

Lynium shook his head. 'Why ask what deep down you already know,' he barked. 'It will come for you, and you'll tell it.' His face collapsed a little. 'Yes and before you ask the next question, your death in this Story will bring the world only a short reprieve. It is however the best option. The real world needs you to fill your space in the third dimension, it will remake you.' He stopped, then added casually. 'Almost as you were when you left.'

'Almost?'

'Yes…,' said Lynium, becoming even fainter. 'This Story's no fool! It will keep something for its trouble, something not composed of matter.' He studied Dreamweaver for a reaction. 'It will snatch at your mind as you leave, Storyteller, and it will retain a generous share. But as you know, it won't call you back. It will wait until another one of your calibre is borne, then the process will begin again. And I must find a way to stop it.'

Dreamweaver smiled, and a tiny trickle of blood drained from the corner of his mouth. 'The Story has made you careless,' he said, 'there's always a third option.'

'Damn you!' choked Lynium. 'This…Story doesn't wax well for either of us…my misery will fan…across the world in a new wave of devastation, and you are the…in..fecti..on. You…must…die…in this…there…is no third…option…'

'If I change the Story, change how it ends, then it all stops here,'

Lynium was a mote-ghost, barely able to hold himself together. 'Noooooo… not possible…. take your own….. life…take… you… will see it is…better… to lose your… mind.'

He watched the last vestige of Lynium vanish. *This really is the work of some morbid genius*, he thought. And it was only now that the full extent of his confrontation surfaced, he could no longer command his legs to bear him up. He fell, throwing out his right arm to soften the impact. He hit the ground.

Unconsciousness claimed him, and part of him was grateful for it. Now – and not for the first time – his fragmented brain had lost its grasp on whether he was dreaming or a character in a new breed of story.

The ambiguity was falling into a new place of making. A place he had never ever expected to encounter in a dream, in a story. Here, the paradox once again. Round and round the thoughts went, in a spiral with Talis at the centre, and he touching her, his lips brushing her sparkling flesh. The shock-wave of her kiss travelling through his mind until it touched his soul's breath. Then his soul bleeding away from his tired body, dissipated and homeless. This was a place in which figments from the human mind met forms from other types of mind.

'I'm scared of you, Dreamweaver,' Talis whispered with mournful breath.

'I imagine the your world opening up to me again, and I desire it.'

'I think your Story is seeping with sadness.'

'A sad story told by something facing its own death.'

Paradox upon paradox, he thought, as his eyes drifted closed again.

Something shook him.

He opened his eyes very reluctantly. He didn't welcome resurrection.

A child was crouched beside him, saying something to him, but his tattered mind couldn't grasp her words. It was a language he'd never heard.

Slowly the words solidified into meaning, and somehow he understood.

'*Wake up,*' she told him. 'You understand me?'

She put her hand on his face; it was warm and soft. Then she bent down and kissed him on the forehead.

'Where am I?' he asked.

She smiled. 'You are here,' she replied.

Her answer rang in his ears. He felt his head on the earth, which was moist and cold, he looked ahead and saw a tree. He saw it upside down; the roots nestled in a bed of clouds, while the golden leaves brushed against the sallow ground. He could make out what looked like plump fruits entwined in the upturned canopy.

He heaved himself onto his hands and knees and crawled incongruously towards the tree. His outstretched hand clasped at the fruit. They looked like apples, except that the skin was metallic, like brushed aluminium. Clearly they were fruit, but no variety he had ever seen. He reached out and picked one, it came from its housing without effort. He sniffed at it. It smelt fermented, like a full-blooded wine. He was too starved to care if it was friendly.

The child grabbed his hand and steered the fruit to his lips, his teeth piercing the volumous skin with ease. The flesh inside had an alcoholic flavour; the juice had a soft, elixirous tinge. He chewed, and the young girl pressed the fruit to his lips for a second bite before he'd swallowed the first, urging him to eat, seeds and all.

Immediately, she brought another to his lips, and he began to devour it with a fierce appetite. He was ravenous. He fed like an animal, not caring as the juice streamed down his neck.

He was feasting when it dawned on him that the ground beneath him was shifting, undulating. He looked up at the child thrusting the fruit at him, but he couldn't quite focus on her. Hell! He'd been poisoned. Lynium had fooled him after all. The remaining fruit dropped from his mouth. He was about to vomit when an extraordinary sensation overtook him.

His surroundings unfurled in a vast scopic vision, its contents seemed hurled at reality like images torn from a picture book. Sizzling auras with bright, deckled edges burst from every plant and granule, laughter billowed from great bruise coloured insects as they lapped at succulent vulvas, and the hypersonic babble of endless thoughts and conversations filled his ears. There were hints of figures moving to either side of him; or was it in him? Anything seemed possible. He concentrated, to get a better grasp of what these things meant. He was being drawn into the knowledge that this state required – celebrated. He could almost feel his flesh crawling through this Story, his mind flipped like gilt-edged pages.

He craned his head back to find the child, and this time she blossomed into focus. Cascades of shiny blue-black hair framed a slim and delicately boned face; she was no more than eight or nine. Her eyes were green, slightly slanted and soulful. She was beautiful: that was his first thought. She was dressed in blues and purples so rich they were alive, the fabric spiralled tightly around her upper body, her young ripeness delicately sealed. Small movements simmered under her skin, shaping a myriad of simultaneous expressions; none of which made any sense; then came a smile.

'The fruit helps strangers see how we see,' she said playfully.

Now, he saw people in the distance, and found he was able to zoom closer and see their features in detail just by thinking it. He pulled himself up, slowly working his new senses.

'Do you eat the fruit?' he asked.

'Oh yes,' replied the girl, squeezing one open. 'It's our custom.'

'What is your name?' he asked gently.

'I'm called Ge~nes,' she said playfully. 'You speak so strangely.'

'I'm known as Dreamweaver, but my real name is Deken. I come from a far away land where we speak different words,' he replied gently.

'Dream – weaver, Dreamweaver, Dreamweaver… I like Dreamweaver, that's a wonderful name,' she said, repeating it over and over.

He smiled, sensitive to the multitude of thoughts wiring through her mind.

'What do you do in this land?' she inquired.

He considered his answer, then said: 'I talk to many people.'

She flicked her blue-black hair innocently, yet it had the makings of a woman.

'Do you tell them stories?' she asked.

Ah! Now he was on surer footing. His eyes sparkled. He would find his way again; the Story was still in his grasp. Lynium's scraping voice echoed in his mind, and in that instant, his resolve strengthened. *For now, I live in a dream*, he thought.

He knelt down and looked into Ge~nes' eyes. 'Yes, I tell stories,' he said softly.

'I have a book that tells me stories,' she said. 'In the dark, in my head, I see them without my eyes. But I am sad.'

'What makes you sad?' he asked.

Ge~nes crumpled her smooth little forehead, deep in thought. 'I want to go to those places. I want to really be there. Terrible things happen and I want to stop them and be there to help the good people and send the evil people away. I think what if – what if I can't find my way out and I die too like my father? He died helping people with the sickness. The wise women say it's impossible to go to these places, because you have to give all your power up just to get there and if you die trapped inside – your mind dies.' Tears spilled from her eyes. 'I don't really understand what that means, I just want to *know* that mother and I will always be safe – and never die.'

Her voice seemed to change. It grew low and masculine. 'You know. Life. Eternal life.'

For a split second the whole scene faltered as if the data that powered it had somehow slipped or jumped. Then all continued as before.

He felt the glitch travel deep into his body. Other forces were at work. He knew he must move quickly. He would not treat this child like some strange contrivance though; he must act with wisdom.

Taking the child by the hand he said: 'I know life is strange, and there are things beyond our understanding. I have no clear answers to give you, Ge~nes, but I offer you this: nothing is ever lost, everything that lives is used to make something new, something unique.'

She computed this information, then, seemingly satisfied, she asked: 'Would you like to read my book, I can take you to it?'

'Yes, I'd like that very much,' he replied.

She tugged at his hand. 'Come on.'

There was a feeling in him then that his body had become the instrument of some power that he could barely control. It threatened to plunge into chaos. He had become a fiction-being, a pretence nestled in blood and nerves, a venomous message in motion. At the core of this fiction-being, he occurred, allowing himself to be led by a child-image. He tried to call his past to mind in an attempt to cauterise the enigma. He tried to feel backwards in time. There was no way to peer into it now, and know that what it contained was true. His life was an illusion from which *he* was absent.

They hurried down a steep slope and along the banks of a gushing river; its waters red like blood, its spume white. A small cinnabar sun shone down through half-stripped branches of trees, and bathed the earth in a glowing, plasmeld pattern.

Presently they came to the brow of a hill and stared down into a city structure hewn from great slabs of yellow rock. What looked like a temple dominated the foreground. Vast hangings along its flanks displayed a single black circle on white. Extravagance butted simplicity; artistry played with tasteless sprawl. People thronged the narrow streets, moving like ants in a strange, intelligent trap.

Ge~nes pointed towards a small cluster of haphazard buildings ensconced behind some trees. 'There,' she said excitedly, 'There.'

They were down in the crush now, people stared, unsure of what to make of this stranger. Their eyes searched his tall, alien structure for clues. He felt exposed. He'd been conditioned to be separate; now he was separate.

He ignored the looks after the first few, there seemed no malice in them, just surprise, maybe fear. He found himself flowing with the crowd, and clasped Ge~nes' hand tightly. She skipped along beside him, through this mnemonic trance, oblivious to her significance.

The noise of an argument broke out from behind. An old voice berated someone. There were sounds of laughter, then young agile feet running. The air was thick with food-like odours.

He'd seen similar sights a thousand times before, but those memories now felt like something that had occurred to another person. For an instant, he felt the touch of adoring crowds; then he was back in the fiction-body. The shifting, acidified present closed around him like a curse and the thought made him smile: a Storyteller trapped in a story.

Ge~nes pushed him towards a small wooden door on their right. She pushed gently down on an old oxidised latch, and the door opened. The gap revealed a warm, sebaceous light. He entered, and heard the door close behind him with a carnal thud.

His senses searched the room. It was small, and opposite the door a wooden table with two chairs sat below a bright hanging. Each chair was friendlied with a small emerald cushion. On the opposite side, a smoky, feminine presence floated in a carved frame. The floor was intricate, beautiful: dotted with bright tiles, depicting exotic goddess-like creatures; the most captivating design was a woman whose flesh was fashioned from flames, dancing, vermilion flames.

A broad shelf precariously clasped at the wall to his right, crammed with books – mostly old and antique looking – some with bright hieroglyphics inscribed on their spines, some in a threadbare condition, almost calcified with age.

He pointed to the books. 'Is your book there?'

Her small, pretty face shone, and the next moment she was balanced on one of the chairs, her rangy little fingers closed around one of the books. She eased the book away from its colleagues, then pirouetted. 'Here, please take it.'

He took the book carefully, and placed it on the table… an instant of hesitation – the animal in him responding. He looked searchingly at what his fiction-fate had delivered: *If this doesn't hold what I need*, he thought. What he needed, he wasn't certain.

On the cover was a pattern of some kind, a design that passed imperceptibly into sound and reconfigured itself over and over. No longer shackled to any reason, he slowly siphoned the hybrid.

It said…

realms of chaos

He opened the book, releasing a spread of skilful illusions. Woooosh :::: A shapeless mass of darkness split apart to reveal the first page, and a frail spindle of light gleamed between his fingers and stroked the brittle paper. In the light, for a moment, there moved a form, a human shape: a woman looking straight into his eyes. Her face was wise and spectral.

'I am here to fulfil a promise,' she said in a voice like rushing water. 'I open the door between worlds, and you will cross the borders of possibility. But remember: possibilities can become worlds.'

She gently imploded back into the paper, and he turned to the next page: this time, he was surprised to see just plain text written in his own language.

{ Dreamweaver – we'll be moving to stranger and more distant places, realms of immeasurable chaos. In these places I cannot protect you – remember – there are only two paths. The first is simple: run from the chaos and it will enshroud and consume you. The second is infinitely more difficult and demands insight and vigilance – focus and learn to recognise who and what, in the midst of the chaos, is not chaos, then believe in this, make it vital and beautiful }

'Talis,' he whispered.

He looked across the table to where Ge~nes was now sitting – she peered at the book expectantly.

The page turned.

At the top of the page the word SEN was emblazoned in thick gold letters, and underneath in a fine eloquent script were the words he'd been waiting for. His eyes scanned the page hungrily; then he began to read out loud.

SEN

Once upon a time, in a far off land called Teloset, there lived a mighty Queen called Namida. Her beauty was that of legend; her skin was as smooth as silk and glowed as white as the finest milk; her eyes sparkled with the purest green like emeralds lit from within. Her hair fell long and straight like a fall of black water.

Yes, yes yes... he thought. *I know this.*

As time passed the Queen became angry and afraid; she saw that her royal beauty was as transient as all things cloaked in flesh, plate or shell. The words 'Death' and 'Age' were banished from the world. She vented her rage upon her subjects, and decreed that every fair maiden and young man be scarred until all trace of youth and beauty was erased.

'Yes.....yes.....yes,' he said.

One day a beautiful Goddess called Sen appeared from the poisoned land in the far reaches of Namida's Kingdom. She came with others she had created from her own radiant flesh. Their wise, sparkling eyes saw much sadness in the people. They travelled the land and used a healing magic to remove the spiteful disfigurements, restoring all to their former beauty. Namida's troops were vanquished in an instant by Sen's mournful singing. They wandered aimlessly, locked in a great trance.

'Yes, this is it,' said Dreamweaver. 'This is it.'

Namida gathered news of these episodes and became enraged. Knowing Sen would come to find her, she would devise a plan.

Only when she had healed the blight, did Sen come before Namida. The Queen was waiting for her in the great hall of her palace, flanked by several sinister-looking guards draped in shinning jet armour.

"You dare to undermine my authority?" bellowed Namida.

Concealing her sadness, Sen bowed so low that her glowing hair touched the floor. "Majesty, I beg your forgiveness, I have been sleeping for a thousand years and I am ignorant of your customs. I simply saw pain and suffering and put an end to it."

Namida studied Sen. "You will give me eternal youth and beauty," she demanded. "I can feel that you possess this power, and as the Queen of Teloset, I command you to act."

"With respect, Majesty, you ask too much," Sen responded. "The Creator has already placed a great treasure within you. The soul is the treasure, the body is the chest, and time is the key that unlocks the chest. There is only one purpose to life: to bear witness to and absorb as much as possible of the complexity of creation, its beauty, its mysteries, its riddles. The more you absorb, the greater will be your enjoyment and your sense of peace. If you have lived a life in joy, you will not be troubled by its ending."

"Silence!" screamed Namida. "You will do as I command!"

Sen remained calm and serene. "I see nothing good from your hand. I see blight upon the land and its people. The arts of men and women forgotten. The artist has no eyes, the singer no tongue. And you command me to give them this forever."

"Do not think that you can out-smart me," snapped Namida. "I have the power to reap great harm if my wish is not granted. The land will run thick with blood. Be warned: do not dream of treachery. Machines will scourge this planet with flames hotter than hell if my heart should ever stop beating." She added, 'The life of a mortal has no value for me."

She put her hand under Sen's beautifully sculpted chin and forced it up so that she could look into her eyes. After she had studied them, she let go of her chin and said: "Perhaps you don't understand. My heart is connected to a terrible force that will destroy everything; obliterate the very essence of vitality."

Sen remained silent for some time; then she spoke. "Majesty, I urge you again to reconsider what you ask. I am immortal, it is true, but I have made healing my soul purpose. There can be no divergence from this path, and I can only pray that our mighty Creator has guided it so." Namida sneered. "And what will you do when you have healed this miserable planet, and there is nothing left for you to heal?"

"I will send this gift to other worlds, and they too will be healed," Sen replied softly.

Namida waved her slim hand at Sen. "Your goddess-mind is flawed," she hissed. "What if they revel in their sickness, and your retched healing denies them this pleasure. Your powers have not granted you access to the ultimate truth. Darkness and death is the treasure that time unlocks. I ask you this: if your Great Creator called down from the heavens, and commanded everyone to be happy from this day forth, what do you think would happen?"

She did not wait for Sen to reply. "Each man would have his own idea of what it meant to be happy, and soon men would slaughter their brothers in the name of happiness." She laughed a terrible hollow laugh. "Power and violence are the fuel of creation. Look into a wolf's eyes as it tears at a deer's throat, and see the spider writhe with pleasure as she devours her foolish lover."

Dreamweaver stopped reading, and looked across at Ge~nes. She smiled innocently.

'Oh please don't stop,' she said in a small, imploring voice. 'It gets very sad.'

'So you've read this story?' he asked.

'Yes,' replied Ge~nes, 'but I cannot seem to remember how it ends. There are some big words that I don't understand. I know it gets very sad though.' She thought for a while. 'They all get very sad,' she said, 'Except I think this one is the saddest of them all.'

He reached across, squeezed her hand. 'Do any of your books have happy endings?'

She crumpled her face. 'I don't think so,' she said, 'And besides, sad stories are much more interesting.'

He nodded. *More interesting*, he thought, *and more dangerous*. He focused again.

Sen shook her head sadly. "It is your mind that is deceived," she said.

Namida's guards cringed.

"You mistake natural aggression for violence," she continued. "Natural aggression provides the charge for all creativity. There is no division between love and natural aggression, they are one and the same. Natural aggression is the 'loving thrust', the way in which love is activated. Through this, creativity is renewed. The wolf and the deer understand the nature of the life-energy they share, and are not jealous for their own individuality. This does not mean that both will not struggle to live, but deep inside they know that they will not be lost."

She turned and gestured out of a great arched window. From below came the sound of trampling feet, from above the thunder of flying machines, and from the distance the cracking of whips against men's backs.

"When men and women understand they will never be lost, they can come out of all this misery, and be free from the torment inside their minds. They can use compassion to shape their actions. When they know that to kill is to be killed, they will preserve creation consciously as the animals do so unconsciously. Men have forgotten this basic fact, and it is only through healing that the veil can be lifted from their eyes..."

Namida held up her hand for silence. Her eyes grew arctic. "Enough, she said. "I've no time for your stupid riddles. Goddesses really aren't what they're cracked up to be. I had hoped that you would see the truth in my words. It is an act of great heresy to speak against your mighty Queen. For this act of treachery many will be tortured and die. I will see to this personally. Now you will give me what I ask.'

Great tears fell from Sen's sparkling eyes, they shattered on the stone floor like carelessly dropped crystals. "No," she pleaded. "No more torture. You have second-guessed me and my Goddess powers cannot move around your will. I will grant you exactly what you ask – eternal life and beauty. But please no more torture and killing."

Namida howled with laughter. "How pitiful, a Goddess crushed."

Yet in her moment of glory, something disturbing flickered across Namida's consciousness. The sweet taste of victory was tinged with a sharp, alien sourness. She had expected to call upon her innermost darkness. Surely it could not be this easy, she thought, I am beeing fooled.

The thought stung her. She became acutely aware. Her eyes moved across Sen's gleaming flesh, she noticed the faint hiss of the tallow candles in their lanterns as they burned bright and steady. The ancient malign faces of glowing californium statues loomed above her. She looked down at herself. Nothing happened. Tiny crumbs of pure diamond glittered dreamily in the silver threads of her skirt like spring raindrops. Still nothing happened; nothing to contradict her power.

Cheers from her sinister guards resounded through the great hall, as crowds of bejewelled sycophants emerged from their hiding places to celebrate the prevalence of their Queen's evil.

The sound of victory washed through Namida, deflecting her thoughts, cleansing her of doubt. Here she stood on the brink of all possibilities; life without death. Immortality. Every soul desires it, she thought, and I will achieve my desire. I will live to see every star rot in the sky as I slip past the workings of atoms!

9

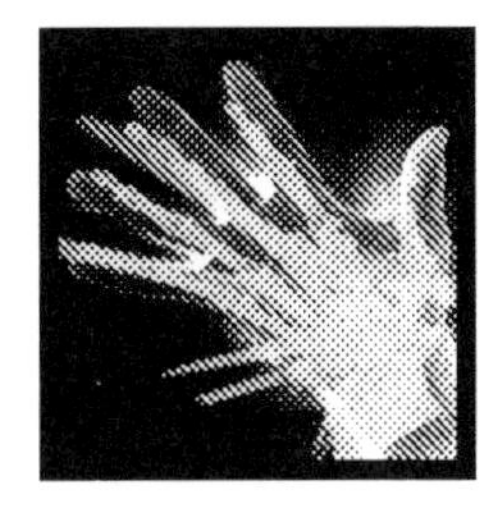

Dreamweaver came to the end of the page. He fingered the small deckled edge reluctantly, brushing the calligraphy with his other hand. Echoes of his voice disappeared into the page like lost memories. Ragged forms were moving across the lettering, so insubstantial he couldn't be sure whether he saw them or merely sensed their presence. Then he turned the page.

A blurred, cold face was melting into the paper, a mask of fluid. Only the cold, lifeless eyes remained distinguishable. He reached to touch the face and it was like plunging his hand into a torrent of ice-water, a torrent swimming with words, fast against the flow; swimming away. He snatched his hand from the flux immediately.

The action released a voice from the page. "Words fall back into time" it said. Then the page stared back crisp, chaste and totally blank.

His breath quickened as he rifled through the rest of the book – knowing deep down there was nothing. The blank leaves flapped through his fingers with shrill laughter.

He shot back in his chair, his hand still smarting from the cold. *The moment of truth*, he thought.

'Oh please, please,' said Ge~nes, 'Don't stop, you read so beautifully.'

'The pages are empty,' he said dejectedly. 'The rest of the book is empty – empty.'

The young girl's face rippled with pleasure. 'That's why I can't remember the end,' she announced triumphantly. Then she leapt from her chair and danced around the room.

His mind simmered, *Think, think, think*.

'Ge~nes!' He shouted. 'Ge~nes, this is very important, and I want you to listen carefully and answer as best you can. Do you understand?'

She slowed to a canter, then stopped. She gazed at Dreamweaver's serious face and suddenly looked tearful. 'Are you angry with me?' she asked. 'Are you angry about the book, because if you are there are other books with stories that have endings? We could read…'

He softened his tone, a nerve twitched at his temple. 'No, Ge~nes, I'm not angry with you or about the book. But it's very important for me to know the rest of the story. Now, do you know why the pages are blank, and is there any way to bring them back to life?'

She looked reassured. 'The book is very old,' she said. 'It belonged to mother, and to grandma before her. Mother said the stories disappear back into time until they are gone.' She gave a big sigh, and puffed out her small, sunset-coloured cheeks. 'This isn't fun anymore, can we do something else?'

He spoke simply. 'Ge~nes, I need your help. But first I will need to tell you a secret so you understand why.'

He smiled, studying the day shadows moving down the wall – thinking. His angular features looked tired from thoughts that hadn't healed, but his eyes still laughed. He didn't want to scare her, say anything he wasn't sure of, and certainly nothing to bring her more sadness.

She stared fixedly at him as if she could learn the secret with her eyes, and he could feel an energy building between them. The beautiful, intriguing symmetry of her fledgling features, and her eyes, her eyes were full of time and sadness.

'You are a dream,' she said. 'I am real and you are the dream.'

For a moment he was shocked. Her voice changed, deep and feminine.

She moved her face slowly. *There's something wrong*, he thought. It didn't feel right, the movement of her hair. She started to laugh. It sounded wrong.

Beads of sweat began to trickle from his brow, and suddenly, he pictured Talis' form. The shape of her naked limbs, the tight purple spreading across them like oil. Her legs in particular – slender – muscular – graceful. He wanted to touch them.

'Do you want me?' she asked.

Time stopped…

He realised the sight of his salacious gaze had frightened Ge~nes into silence. She was just watching him, and the look on her face was distressing to see. He lowered his head into his hands, feeling ashamed and somehow tarnished by this Story. It was twisting him into a mixed message, and for the first time in many years a raw, primordial anger rose up and gripped every part of him. His fists clenched – eyes roared.

She backed away, unsure, disturbed. 'I know there is something wrong and I'm afraid to know what it is,' she said in a shaky voice. 'I know you are in trouble and my mother says it is good to help people when they are in trouble. I don't know if you are bad. I don't think you are. You are so different and beautiful like the characters in the stories. I like it when the stories have no endings. It's like they go on forever and the characters go on forever and I will never get old and be grown-up and die…die…die…' her voice echoed into the distance.

He raised his head, and tears ran down his cheeks. 'Please, don't be afraid, Ge~nes. I didn't mean to frighten you. The truth is I'm lost and confused.' He squeezed composure into his mind. 'Will you help me, Ge~nes?'

She stared at him through a veiled confusion. Then she tentatively edged forward and took his hand. Her miniature fingers felt so light and fragile. 'I…I will help you,' she said unsteadily. 'M… Mother has h… heard how the story ends.' She hesitated. 'It was a long time ago… but she remembers things before I was born and she remembers Grandma as a young woman.'

He felt her fear release, layer by layer. It came to rest. 'Can you take me to your mother?' he asked softly. 'Will she come home soon?'

She shook her head. 'She serves at the great Temple and when the Life-Crystals speak the servers must stay. No one is allowed inside unless they serve. You look so strange they will never let you in. I think that you will be in even greater trouble.'

He reached over and clasped her hand, and she let him do it.

'Ge~nes, I must speak with your mother. Is there any way?'

She plunged into thought. Time passed. Then she said: 'I can give you Father's robe and some of his normal clothes and his hat. He's been dead for many years and I don't think he will mind. The clothes will make you less handsome and the robe will cover your head and the guards will think you are a server. Remember not to put the robe on until you are almost at the temple. The guards know me but we must not be seen together. I will slip in first and tell Mother you need her help.' Then she added casually. 'Oh, I almost forgot: you will need to pass through the Soul-Scanner.'

He felt his heart katabase like a lift with no brakes. 'Soul-Scanner?' he said in a bleak voice.

She smiled impishly. 'Don't worry – because Mother is a Server she was permitted to keep Father's Soul-Crystal. It contains the imprint of his soul. He was also a Server and his essence is still stored in the temple so it will let you pass through the scanner. I have used it to creep into the temple and listen to the Priestess' chanting.'

She went to the far end of the room and slid something from a hollow in the wall, and came back clutching a small, golden casket in both hands. Then placing it gently on the table, she stepped back and said: 'There it is.'

Dreamweaver peered down at the casket as it gleamed with lavish abandon, and it seemed strangely out of place in the small, spartan interior. He noticed the lid was decoratively etched, and he lingered over it, inspecting its concealed subtleties. It depicted the kind, bearded face of a man in his middle years. His eyes were large and expectant with the same small slant as Ge~nes carried on her eyes.

'I think I would have liked your father,' he said.

Ge~nes brushed her hand over her father's eyes, they gently closed, and the casket sprang open. A tiny crystal body lay embalmed in a matrix of sparkles.

'Father, I would like you to meet my very special friend, Dreamweaver,' she said formally.

The artistry was exquisite, so detailed and delicate that he half expected it to sit up and talk. He craned over the miniature body like a colossus. 'A pleasure to meet you, sir,' he said.

She giggled. Then she suddenly looked concerned. 'This is our most treasured possession, Dreamweaver. I trust you to keep it safe.'

'I'll keep it safe,' he said.

'When you pass through the scanner,' continued Ge~nes, 'you must hold it to your heart and the structure will let you pass. As you walk through, some of Father's memories and thoughts will come into your mind and you will think they belong to you, so don't be afraid if you feel different - Mother often takes his soul and I watch her walking in and out of the scanner with tears running down her face. I did it once but I didn't understand his thoughts – I think they had something to do with love.'

He smiled.

'...Now what have I forgotten?' she pondered. '...Oh yes! If you are caught it might be better to kill yourself. I've heard what happened to someone they caught in the temple and it was the most horrible thing ever – and when his Soul-Crystal was made they kept it somewhere dark and full of spiders.'

'Then I must make absolutely sure I don't get caught,' said Dreamweaver in a serious voice.

She adopted the more business-like tone. 'I will go first and you will follow on. Remember to take the main street. You must enter through the front door. When you are inside take great care to cover your face, the Structures are very observant. You must not give anything away.'

'How will I find your mother?' he asked.

'Mother is called Te~nes. You must go to the Life-Crystals next to the altar and touch Father's soul against the point of the largest crystal. She will come for you.' With this she made her way to the door. She turned and studied Dreamweaver's eyes wondering what they saw.

'Can I be in one of your stories?' she asked sweetly.

He stretched out his arms as if to call her back, then lowered them. He couldn't take his eyes off her, vibrant and fragile in this sanctuary, this little, shabby sanctuary.

'You already are,' he said. 'You already are.'

'Remember to pull the hat down as low as you can,' she said. 'People change when the sun goes down so they will be more suspicious.'

At the last moment she turned. 'Gone,' she said.

This time he resisted the temptation.

10

Dreamweaver waited some time before setting out.

He had used the time to wash in a tiny bathroom – too small for him to stand upright – and discard his old, tattered clothes. He'd sensed the corpus of Earth in their threads, making him hesitate before letting them go. Suddenly a memory-cloud had vapoured his mind – the looks of superstitious awe calcified on peoples' faces on the day he'd left his home, the way they'd gently parted in silence to let him through, and the feather-light touch of their hands against his body. He'd stared at his body in the mirror: taught, muscular, slender... a few marks of battle: but essentially the same as that day. Looking up, he'd studied his face – large image-drinking eyes; the focused eremite features of inner solitude. He noticed something new though: a vulnerability seeping through his countenance, a fragile power – so still, so vulnerable.

Something his mother had once said slipped into his mind:

'Viewed from a distance, our lives form patterns – beautiful patterns – which fit perfectly into the Universe. Even the most wretched life is beautiful and fits perfectly. Nothing that happens, no matter how surface-flawed, can ever move outside the beauty of the pattern.'

For a moment, he'd seen her wise, crinkled eyes and the tissue-flesh of her delicate hands as they tatted songbirds and flowers. He contemplated all the wonderment and violence housed within this Story. It came... it went... songbirds and violence... it came... it went...

The clean, crisp clothes felt luxurious against his skin: a white, silk shirt and linen trousers to match. He pulled on the hat and smiled to himself, placing the little gold casket carefully in his pocket, he tucked the robe under his arm, and walked out into the twilight aura of the street.

The light was fading and the creeping movements of life had taken on a new dimension. He moved like a shadow-creature across a small plaza which led to the main street. Structures glimmered in the ghostly half-light. Steam spiralled off rooftops. Small children played across the way, throwing sticks into a tree, then running to catch the tumbling fruit.

He turned onto the busy thoroughfare and found it crammed with people. He moved through the throng, wasting no time surveying the varied parade of creaturehood on display; there was much to see though. Windows flickered with fiery, strobe-frozen harlots, malodorous beasts twisted on open spits – plaited with colourful bastings. A mingle of shrieks and prayers convulsed from thin cones mounted along the street and merged effortlessly into the dense, operatic striving.

His senses absorbed the scene without pulling him from his purpose. A heartbeat later, the attention he'd so carefully avoided hit him like an accusation.

A withered old woman, bent almost double by injury or affliction, stepped shakily into his path. The collision sent a random pattern of pedestrians sprawling to the ground, and his hat following behind them.

There was something ritualistic in the way the figures tumbled over and over. There was a flash of light, then a hissing, screaming sound – a crunch of flesh against stone. Someone went sliding past to his right, and when he turned to look, he could see more people tumbling over, trying to balance but still falling, screaming – blood pumping from a woman's face. It was a movement contagion – a display of such comical extravagance that he almost laughed.

Then a tracer beam swept over the scene, and a siren rang out from the tiny speakers that only hours before had sung prayers.

But there was worse to come. The old woman was now struggling to her feet, covered in blood and dirt, pointing an accusing finger at him.

'Him!!' she shrieked. 'It was him! Look at him, look at him, he's a devil – look how strange he looks... Devil!!!!!!!'

Then another woman, young and pretty this time, flung herself at him, ready to scratch out his eyes. He stumbled back, crashing into more people as she came after him.

'Demon!' she yelled. 'Evil one!'

Somebody behind him shouted: 'Kill him!' An instant later a cacophony of screams all baying for blood resounded through the crowd. Then came the first missile. It hit him on the side of the face, gouging a deep trench through his cheek, but before the pain had a chance to register, a second missile struck. Then a third hit his shoulder. The surging mass of people came under the influence of the spectacle. He was trapped in an amphitheater of hate and bodies, as everyone turned on him. He knew the issue was life and death.

Frightened by their own imaginings, this mob was going to tear him to pieces. He looked around for an escape route; a small street to his left offered the merest vestige of hope.

Then a jagged stone struck him on the forehead sending him to the floor, writhing in pain, blood gushing from a deep wound. The golden Soul-Casket flew from his pocket and skidded across the ground. He flung himself after it, fingers ploughing the dirt. A strong, manicured hand reached down and collected the treasure, just as a foot snared his wrist to the ground.

He looked up, searching for a face to fit the hand. Everything was just a blaze of fractals, no longer flesh. 'Noooo!' he screamed. Darkness began to fuse the scene together, and then the explosion of gunfire. A body was blown back, fractals exploding, all across his face. A second bullet struck him in the arm, it went straight through, pitching him forward, so that his face was pressed flat against the dirt and stone, spittle and blood flying, and he was just lying there waiting for his back to explode, and the wilderness to suck on his imbecilic mind.

Quite suddenly, the bedlam ceased, as a woman in a military uniform broke through the lynch mob. Several lynchers were already protesting.

'He's a demon, Mistress,' said one individual, a young boy clutching a large, bloodied stone who, before the stone had called to his hand, might have been a shoeshine.

'We must kill the evil one,' demanded a smartly dressed young woman with blood streaked across her face.

The uniformed woman walked up to where he was lying and emptied a third bullet into her victim. He let out an agonised scream.

Turning to the mob she screamed, 'He's a prisoner of the Temple, and will be executed in the Method, now go on your way!'

More sirens broke the spell, and members of the mob began to shake their heads, dislodging the jihad fever.

The trampled corpse of a dog lay steaming in the gutter.

A vestigial protest shimmered through the crowd, but most decided to slope away before they were detained.

The Agent pushed the barrel of her gun into his back. 'Can you stand?' she asked, and turning to the remaining stragglers. 'Goooooo!!!!!!!!,' she screamed.

They reluctantly obliged, cursing as they went.

'Can you stand?'

Dreamweaver's voice came through as if it was beamed from another galaxy. '…I…d……. on't think… so.'

'Don't waste time thinking then, just do it now,' ordered the woman. 'Do you want my blood on your hands too?… Get up… walk!'

A brutalised face turned up and looked deep into her strong eyes.

The cacophony of sirens grew closer and closer.

'Get up,' said the woman, 'I can't be seen to help you, we've only got about a minute to live if you don't move.'

He let out a long, shuddering breath. He forced it – not the best way – but somehow he walked. Shadows walked with him in place of people, his being was collapsed, a system of chaos. The gun pushed through his skull, steering him into the nexus...

Darkness dropped like a black-out curtain....

11

The face was a tangled contrivance, the body an irreconcilable waste that clung to the delicate thread of life. But most of it didn't understand how to live any more, by degrees his body was slowly cleansing itself of life, of time.

The effort to keep lids open was too much, so what was left of Dreamweaver drifted in darkness. Waking and sleep were much alike now: sleep invaded by stories and pain, wakefulness crammed with pain and unanswered questions drifting back into dream-like configurements.

His wracked body lay under soft sheets, and the pain was intermittently eclipsed by a woman's voice. He sometimes heard her bargaining with death on his behalf, and wanted to tell her that it was fine to let him go. But he couldn't move his lips.

Later came a second voice, softer, more delicate. It flowed like a memory-fleck through his mind.

'Will he die?' the soft voice asked.

'I think he will go soon,' said the first voice mournfully.

'Then you must tell him,' said the soft voice. 'It is what he would wish.'

'I don't think he will hear me.'

'He will know,' insisted the soft voice. 'I'm sure he will know.'

'Go now,' said the first voice. 'Go to the hills and bring me the fruit – go… hurry.'

In the velvet darkness Dreamweaver was certain he was a story told by someone else. There was no future in him, and no past. His chest had folded in on him. Wounds on his face and body no longer tried to heal. He could not shift the pain any more because it encased him; it clung to him in a suicide pact between two forbidden lovers. He felt his body parting from the room; it had lost its pull on him. He tried to picture what had happened, but pain wiped the images from his mind. *If there is a God*, he thought, *he is ruthless and totally blank – all life is a terrible illusion - and even death carries no freedom from it all: never born, never die – the greatest illusion of them all.*

He voyaged between thoughts separated by parsecs, eternity in the blink of an eye. The face of a beautiful woman came to him in the midst of this lingering void, shimmering like moonlit water. *The more you feel like you belong*, she sang, *the less you must belong*. The thoughts drifted like shadows in smoke, weightless, meaningless…

Time stood frozen… something touched his lips. A glassy light passed through him: death turning back into life. A voice blistered through the vacuum, soothing, uninterrupted. He saw the sound moving towards his mind…

'Namida, the evil Queen of Teloset had played her hand against Sen, the beautiful Goddess,' said the voice…

Faced with the destruction of all Teloset and its people, Sen had conceded to grant Namida eternal youth and beauty.

Sen had two huge dilemmas to address in one stroke. First, she needed to ensure that the evil Queen's heart would never stop beating and so trigger the machines of hideous destruction. Sen could see the machines with her powerful psyche, feel each one as it lay immersed in a cold malevolence that sensed her presence, and peered into her mind. Even Sen's healing touch was scorched as it probed this energy. She dare not underestimate Namida, and giving her immortality would deal with this immediate threat. The second dreadful dilemma would ripen once Namida was immortal. Sen needed a means to quell this scourge unleashed upon eternity.

Being a Goddess carried great responsibility. Many had fallen short of the mark and abused their powers. But Sen fostered wise and creative thoughts, and a plan took seed in her radiant mind: a special condition would be woven into the blueprint of Namida's immortal framework...

"Hurry! Hurry!" Snapped Namida impatiently.

Sen collected her thoughts, then placed a hand inside her belly and drew out a ball of gleaming flesh. The ball sprouted stalks, growing, locking together into the shape of Namida's body. Sen had the pattern in her eyes and she was sculpting with thoughts. The new likeness of Namida was as young and beautiful as she had been all those years ago. It shimmered against the light like a silver ghost.

"I must be even more beautiful than before!" screamed Namida.

No sooner had she spoken than the likeness became even more vivid and beautiful, and the palace guards fell to their knees in awe.

When Sen had finished constructing the eternal garment, it floated freely in front of the horrid, sadistic Queen.

"Yes, yes, yes," said Namida; "This is how I will be forever. I will intoxicate everything, and in the passing of time, nothing will evade my understanding, nothing will escape my influence."

Sen smiled a knowing smile. "Majesty, it is time for you to step into your new vestment."

Hungry for such dazzling beauty and confident that she had truly subjugated Sen, Namida stepped gracefully into her splendid semblance and shuddered with delight. It closed around her ageing, hate-fuelled body like a skin shedding backwards and the new Queen stood resplendent.

The sinister guards ran to grovel at her feet.

Namida beamed down at them. "You will go out into the world and spread the wondrous news of my transformation, tell how I am now the Goddess of Teloset, more beautiful and powerful than Sen."

Sen smiled and waited for Namida's attention. "Majesty, now I have granted your wish, I must instruct you upon the maintenance of your new form," she levied.

Namida glared at Sen and began to feel dizzy. "What absurdity is this?" she screamed. "Conditions? There can be no conditions!!" she howled.

A spectral glow encircled Sen's head. "Namida, your greed and violence has snared you in a trap of your own making. As a Goddess of healing I must always act in accordance with my purpose. Therefore, I have granted you the gift of eternal youth and beauty with the clause of healing as its fulcrum."

"Healing!!?' bellowed Namida. 'Healing!!????'

"You forget, Namida," said Sen, "I was once a mortal, pregnant with time and mortal thoughts. Yet it is only as a Goddess that I have signed the fate of men with their own blood.

For each soul that I have taken from flesh, I have suffered ten-fold the pain I have caused. Therefore I inflict upon you no more than I carry in my own immortal being."

She opened her arms in a gesture of accord. "You will therefore receive tenfold all pain that you inflict on any of the Great Creator's creatures, you will feel even the minutist suffering. Every discretion will leave its mark upon your now perfect body. But I enclose a great gift within this clause, one that I myself do not possess. The pattern works both ways. For every act of love that you perform, you will be blessed tenfold with the joy of the recipient. This will bathe your beauty in the splendour of the Great Creator and replenish it. So you will see that I have given you the mechanism for eternal beauty, and you are its keeper."

'Aaaaaaaaahhhhhhhhhh!!!' screamed Namida 'I will destro....**
G........u............Destr...........

I....()))))))))))))...

(?)...(?)

'Oh God – Oh no! He just died...'

'No... no... no... He can't die, he can't die... I won't let him die.'

'Come now, leave him to sleep with God... come.'

'No, no, he can't be dead, he didn't finish the story...'

'Time takes back its children, my love. Now, let the Sisters prepare the Crystal. They must take great care to record his soul; there's not much time. We must place him before the sun rises.'

12

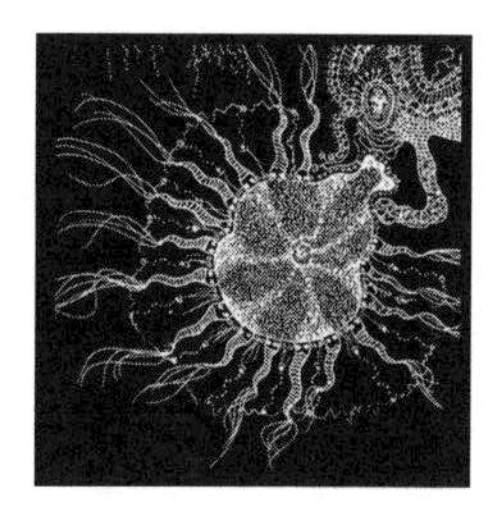

Dreamweaver was at his desk...he gently coaxed the tiny, spinning Mer-Ka-Ba from his lips. With the power of thought, he guided it back into the Word Vessel placed on his desk.

'You have the story?' came a soft, feminine voice from behind.

He turned to look at her.

He smiled, and reached for her hand. She drew it away as though his touch would scald her delicate flesh.

'You said you would bring it back,' she snapped. 'The Elders say you must tell it to the world, that it contains a message for us.'

'I can't remember it,' he said. He watched her face. 'I can't remember how it ends.'

He plucked the Word Vessel from his desk and held it up to the light. 'Every day there's less and less. It just slips away like salt in water.'

'Yes so you keep saying,' snapped the young woman impatiently. 'But you said you would bring it back from the wilderness, and now I'm afraid, not only will they kill you if you don't bring it back, but they will kill me too if they can. I can't even go outside any more. They just sit there, thousands of them, just sitting there, waiting, day after day... waiting. And you, what do you do: just sit there while it drains from your mind?'

Dreamweaver turned to face her angrily. 'Look, I've told you, something happened to me out there. I had the Story… I had it… '

He clasped his head with both hands. 'Somehow, I don't have the same mind anymore, it feels empty and cavernous. Words scowl at me from dark little corners. They won't come out, they just won't come out. I'm not the damned Dreamweaver any more; don't you get it… don't you get it?'

Tears streamed down his tired, handsome features. 'Let me tell you what happened in the wilderness.'

She covered her ears. 'No. No. I don't want to know what happened out there.'

'I think it might help things, please.'

'Just finish the story, damn you. Damn you to hell!

She wept. 'I thought you would come back, and they would love you even more for what you have done for them, but now they begin to despise you. They say you were a trickster all along. They melt your stories in the streets.'

'SIT DOWN AND LISTEN!'

She sat.

'I want you to hear me, hear me this last time. I need to go back, go back and try and find the Circle again.'

'You really have lost your mind, they'll never let you go. They'd rather see you dead.'

'What difference does it make any more. They'll find a way to strip me out whatever happens. This isn't for them any more, I've done enough, God knows, I've done enough. This time it's for me. Now listen carefully. I want you to get out of here, go to the place we always talked about. Take as many Crystals as you need, take them all. I won't need them where I'm going.'

He thought for a moment. 'But I need you to stay a while longer though. You'll need to keep talking as if I'm still here, open a window and keep talking.'

'Dreamweaver, I'm really scared! How will you get out of the city?'

'Let me worry about that. Just be careful, trust me and keep well. If I make it, we'll all laugh about it some day.'

'I'm sorry for what I said. It's just that I get so afraid of all those people, all wanting something from you, all wanting you to solve their problems with the Story. I know it won't make them better...I just don't understand any more.'

She leaned forward, looking into his eyes. 'Dreamweaver, I can see you're not the same as you were. You left something in that circle. But I still have what's left now. If you go back it may take everything.'

'You know me well by now, it's always been all or nothing,' he said.

She pulled him to her. 'Go, safe my love, go safe. I'll wait for you. Then no more Stories, eh.'

He kissed her gently. She closed her eyes.

'Healer,' she said. 'Hands of a Healer from now on. Gone...'

'Gone.'

13

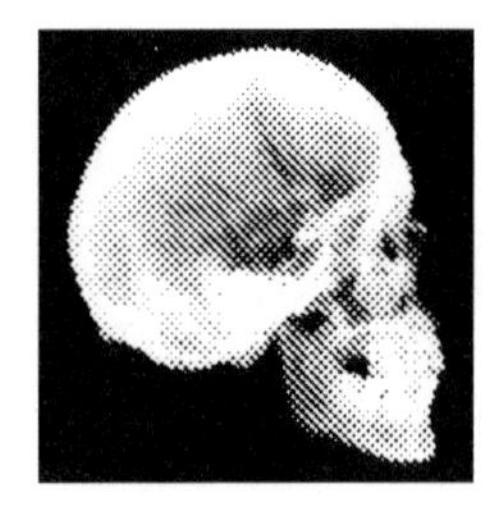

Dreamweaver placed his feet on the edge of the circle. His face was taut and the wind hit it like a fist. Small flies darted across the earth as scorpions danced and killed in the scrub. His only witnesses, insects and the wind.

He waited…

Suddenly, something thudded onto the sand next to his right foot. He looked down at the small golden casket.

He bent to pick it up. A voice came from behind.

'Tut, Tut, Tut… careless, very careless, Dreamweaver, she trusted you. And really, that whole episode in the street...'

Dreamweaver remained still, looking at the picture on the casket. 'I'm beginning to think that you're not a very nice man, Lynium,' he said coldly, then placed the casket into his pocket. 'Tell me, just out of curiosity, who was the woman that pulled me out of the street?'

He looked up to see Lynium standing on the opposite side of the circle.

'Oh her,' said Lynium. 'Clever woman, nasty little incident with her daughter though.'

Dreamweaver smiled. 'That was cheap, really cheap… You were saying…'

Lynium brushed his chin as if he was drawing out the information from some incredibly deep place. 'Now where was I? Oh yes... As it turned out, news travels fast and she got wind of the commotion all the way up there in the Temple, put two and two together, and came up with you. The kid had filled her in by then. She went down to the guardhouse, and walked out with a couple of items, shall we say. I tried to stall her, of course, but she's really quite good.'

'Too bad I never got to meet her,' said Dreamweaver. 'But I enjoyed the whole drama of escaping from the city and journeying to this place again. I really felt my mind had gone, that was very well done Lynium. And all those days trying to remember a Story that I haven't even finished learning yet. Very good.'

Dreamweaver turned and started to walk away.

'Where do you think you're going?' Lynium called after him. 'There's nowhere to go.'

Dreamweaver stopped, and a scorpion scuttled under a rock. The sun burnt into his neck. 'There's one thing I don't understand,' he said.

'What's that?' asked Lynium.

'I thought you said that if I died in the story, really died, with all the pain, then I would end up back in the wilderness with half my mind sucked out? Well, I'm still here.'

Lynium's dark, joy-deserted eyes peered down into the Circle. 'Yes, that was annoying. I'm not entirely sure. As you can imagine, I don't want to give anything away, but it had something to do with that annoying kid. Somehow you were on the way out when she pulled you back.' He frowned. 'But you can rest assured, it won't happen again. I'll see to it personally.'

With this, Dreamweaver turned and walked back to the Circle. He met Lynium head-on, fixing him in his gaze. 'I know this is all some mad piece of fiction, but I'm warning you now: harm a single hair on that child's head and...'

'And... what... I'm dead?' sneered Lynium. 'But I'm already dead, I died five hundred years ago. You can't kill a figment, Mr. Storyteller.

My job is simply to ensure that you fail, that's all, and if that means killing the child, then...'

'I'll find a way to kill you all over again,' interrupted Dreamweaver.

The wind cut between them, they stayed locked. The sun beat down, and the counterfeit wilderness hummed with flies. Small pieces of scrub blew into the Circle and instantly disappeared.

Eventually, Dreamweaver turned and began walking in the opposite direction.

Lynium called after him again. 'You don't know how the myth ends, you can't go on.'

Again, Dreamweaver stopped. 'Yes I do,' he said.

Suddenly, Lynium grasped his head, falling to his knees in apparent agony. He screamed. 'Damn you, Storyteller.' A voice crashed through his head like a missile.

For what seemed like an eternity, she looked deep into the Goddess's eyes, and for a second she hesitated. 'I.... Lo... v... y...' she seemed to stammer, then gave up.

Like a thrusting rapier all the women flew at her, eyes blazing. But the Repugnance made no attempt to evade them, simply closing her fingers around the heart.

A blinding flash. Searing heat. Vaporised flesh.

The blemished sphere rocketed out through the dome, hurtling into the heavens...

Lynium fell face-down, gasping.

'She was very insistent about me remembering,' he said. 'She told me to come back to it if I became lost. Plus, I'm beginning to learn a few tricks of my own.'

Lynium staggered to his feet. He was starting to fade just as he'd done before, his jet-black clothes becoming decidedly grey in appearance. He reached into his jacket and pulled out a book with a black cover, and what looked like a painting enclosed in a square positioned in the centre of the page.

He tossed it through the air and it landed at Dreamweaver's feet.

'This is where it all goes wrong for you, Storyteller,' he shouted. 'This is where you find out that you're not what you thought you were. From now on, you're lost, I mean really lost. Up until this point it's all been a bit cosy, don't you think, like some nice little adventure where the hero's working his way through this Story… Well forget it!'

Now it was Lynium's turn to go. In a matter of seconds he was practically transparent. 'I know how much you enjoyed the whole book thing with that damned kid,' he shouted from thin air. 'So I thought I'd give you the bad news in a nice smart book. Go on, don't be shy! Pick it up! Have a read…….'

Laughter imploded into thin air……………

Dreamweaver picked up the book and read the words on the cover.

THE SEED

BY DEKEN NOS-ANTIMON

He opened it to the first page and read out loud.

The taste of death is less bitter than 'life' without ending. In the stream, which bleeds from the emerald silence of eternity, you will forget and again seek the illusion of time. It is then that the endless moment is lost, and you must breathe again. And if nothing ever comes to lift you from the damp earth and walk you back into the light, then you will truly sleep as never before.

The Seed Singer

He closed the book and stood perfectly still. The wilderness spanned before him vast and inexplicable. He was tired and confused, but no longer a wilderness innocent. The illusion was complete and fastidious. The burning scrub was a barren and malicious host, indiscriminating in its harshness. Even the dream-cast lizards seemed to suffer at its hand.

He observed the vista. It seemed that time stood still, and the soul of the real world had let him go forever. He was reduced to an interloper, lost within an impostor universe. *No matter*, he thought.

He stared down at the Circle, *not this time*, he whispered, *not this time*. Turning, he walked away until it faded into the distance, and only the wind and Lynium's voice echoed in his mind.

He walked for hours, tired, thirsty and hungry. His lips became dry, and blistered like flaking pastry, his head pounded, and gradually the strength was deserting his legs, yet he felt strangely resolved. Despite Lynium's attempts to wrong-foot him, he possessed the foundations to the Story. Now his thoughts flew like wind blowing in many directions, and he sifted their eddies for clues, any clues.

So far, most of the Story had centred around the weird and catastrophic events on Teloset. The story of Namida's fanatical quest for immortality and her ensuing rage against beauty, the distant genesis of Sen as the Goddess of healing, and the cataclysmic convergence of these seemingly disparate elements.

Images from the original visions were falling into their lurid compartments. He now placed meaning upon the miraculous tribe of women, and understood how Sen's ruined vessel was blasted into an unsuspecting Universe by Namida's final gesture of hatred. But as for Talis' role in the story, the ominous presence of Peter Lynium, and the meaning behind the kaleidoscope of other visual elements, there were still only questions. Then came the biggest question of them all: how had this Story been erased from the Earth's psyche?

To understand the whole picture… yes… yes… that was it…. he needed to tie all these elements together. Move through them systematically.

He smiled. *Storyteller turns detective*, he thought…

He tracked back to Talis' words:

'In the visions you've gazed upon a time lost in the Earth's memory, a time of wonderment and miracle, but also a time of immeasurable tragedy, desire…'

And what message was encrypted into the Story's linear façade?

'Through your lips the story hidden in this Circle will again taste life and blood and breathe. From your lips it will shape itself into a Legend – you will speak it – speak it in the magical tongue.'

His mind cruised over the other elements…

It wasn't difficult to deduce that Sen's tarnished vessel had landed on Earth and spawned its tribe of Sen replicas, the Sirens. Likewise, it wasn't a great leap of imagination to suspect these supervenes of possessing more than a hint of Namida's darkness.

Possible clues to the other elements in the visions lay at the heart of the Sirens' deviation from Sen's original Application. The heaven-realm, the Warrior-Race, all this outside the programme, fodder for the tale, meat on the bones…

What was it she'd said…?

'After the Sirens appeared on Earth, they self-fertilised their bodies, creating a race of immortal warriors to act as their consorts and the guardians of the "Spirit Technology". Together they surrounded the Earth with an entirely new realm untrammelled by entropy and time.'

Then, there was the gift of immortality to the chosen few. Now that was definitely the mechanism of darker forces. From what he had seen of events, Sen had intended a gift of healing, not a shortcut to eternity, a free ride to Godhood.

His mind scanned back into Ge~nes' book, The Realms Of Chaos:

"With respect, Majesty, you ask too much," Sen responded. "The Creator has already placed a great treasure within you. The soul is the treasure, the body is the chest, and time is the key that unlocks the chest. There is only one purpose to life: to bear witness to and understand as much as possible about the complexity of existence – its beauty, its mysteries, its riddles. The more you understand, the greater will be your enjoyment and your sense of peace. If you have lived a life in joy, you will not be troubled by its ending."

He thought back…

'The frail human condition was granted the prerogative of the Gods and given the chance to transcend into a sparkling void of never-ending stimulation. Immortality!'

Now there was another element: this new book. He stopped walking. He didn't intend to read it until he was in a more comfortable setting. And then, he needed to take great care.

The heat blasted his face. His mouth felt as dry as fire. He looked down at the cover. He studied the image. It depicted Talis kissing her own refection, set against a huge crimson and silver sun. He read the type again. The Seed, by Deken Nos-Antimon. Insight swept through him. The book contained something he needed. *What price for this*, he thought?

He was meant to find the book somewhere along the way, he was absolutely sure. He thought carefully. *Yes!!! Yes! That's it.* He'd never seen Lynium create anything new in any of the environments he'd materialised in.

He thought….

Yes. So the book existed as part of the Story's interface. Lynium couldn't actually create anything new. Talis had this capacity, but Lynium wasn't part of the interface, he was something else, something dislodged from the Story, a rogue cell, a cancer.

He conjured up Lynium's words..

'This is where it all goes wrong for you, Storyteller.
This is where you find out you're not what you thought you were.'

Clever, he mused. He can't create anything new, but he can move things around – take things from one setting and place them in a different setting. He'd done it with the casket. Dreamweaver smiled.

The casket. That sweet, little object - was it the crucial clue? Lynium had unwittingly revealed his method. *The book came from another part of the Story*, he laughed, *and Lynium made sure I received it too soon*.

He thought again… Wait a minute. He looked down again. *The Seed*, he read… *by Deken Nos-Antimon*. Deken…?

The wind began to gust. It circled round him, searching for a hold. He needed to rest, but the wilderness made no provisions for such niceties. This was a place of things moving, of sand flowing, insects biting and clouds disappearing. Sounds drifted towards him like ghost-lovers, calling him, pushing their touchless flesh to his face, to his hands. In his mind, they danced around him mockingly, knowing he was powerless to stop them. The scrub became fertile with bareness, ripened on emptiness.

He called into the dust. 'Talis, Talis.'

The wind howled…

Soon the scrub was swirling in dust so thick that he lost all perspective of near and far. A sheet of soft umber rose up before him. His world shrunk to the width of an outstretched arm.

The wind screamed…

He edged forward, blind and lost. He laughed at his own arrogance, his belief that this ghost-infested wilderness would open into his next path. He cursed himself for walking away from the circle. *Why didn't I step back inside*? he asked, over and over? Only god-men, fevered on prayer, flourish in the wilderness; unravelled from reality, feasting on visions and eternity. The wind lifted him, trying to part him from his body. He tried to swim in it. He tried to exorcise it from his mind. His fingers let go of the book; it fell into the sand. He fell into the sand.

Down… down… down… Talis… Talis…

Her eyes were crammed with dreams. It felt good to be near her again. She smiled over her shoulder. She was naked and the tiny crystal shrine glistened with a fine coating of morning dew beside her. Dreamweaver edged over to the little shrine, and peered into his refection, staring at what he looked like. of what he could remember…

The trees swayed gently in the breeze, and he sat back looking up at the sky. Clouds drifted past unaware they were being observed from below. Their world one of vapours and wind. not flesh and thoughts.

'Dreamweaver, you remembered the shrine. Do you remember how I told you to keep it in your mind.'

He stared into his own eyes as they reflected in the billions of facets. 'Why must I remember this more than anything else?'

Talis reached forward and tenderly took his hand. 'I… I… I don't really know,' she said shakily. 'I just know it's very important for you and for… I… I … Strange, I can't seem to see the images.'

'If it makes you happy, I'll keep it safe in my thoughts,' he said.

She spoke casually. 'I've missed you, Dreamweaver. You seem like a memory.'

'Like a memory of something that can never happen, but you see it so clearly, as if you were there and living it, feeling it, tasting it.'

'There's a desire in you, Dreamweaver,' she whispered in a mournful voice, 'to do something that changes everything. But I sense great danger ahead, and it chills me to the core.'

'Why have you left me in this dream for so long?' he asked. 'This is still the same dream-sequence?'

'You were pulled away, I tried to get you back, but you just went...'

'His name is Lynium, Peter Lynium. He pulled me away. Tell me about him.'

'I can't tell you, Dreamweaver. It's as if the words and images just won't rise from the depths of my mind.'

He stared into her eyes. 'It's Lynium that's sabotaging me in this story. I need to know why. Think, Talis… think.'

'Dreamweaver, If I had the answers I'd...'

He smiled, running a hand through his hair. His eyes seemed to shine with the same preternatural light which spilled from Talis. He was falling deeper into the arms of the Story. He was living again as a dream within a dream. Part of a fiction-being was dying in the scrub, just as another fiction-being stared at her beautiful face.

'I sense something bad Talis,' he said. 'There's something dark pulling your strings.' He hesitated. 'Look, I didn't quite mean it like it sounded. What I meant was, I feel you're being used somehow. You're an interface filled with hidden thoughts, and it doesn't make sense to me.'

She became thoughtful. 'You can never go back to the real world and be happy with the workings of time. That's why you must deliver the Story, Dreamweaver.'

'In stories the dead walk as the living, but the real world isn't a story. People stay dead, or wounded by life, they cannot die and simply think themselves back into life. They're gone, really gone. In the Story, your magic works but...'

She looked very sad. 'So I finally meet the man of my dreams and he tells me I'm not real enough.'

'Now you're being clever,' he said.

She remained still. Tears ran down her face.

He took her tear-stained face between his hands, and very lightly, very gently, kissed her. She sat motionless, her eyes closed.

Finally she opened her eyes and looked at him with a smoldering, tranced-out gaze.

'I'll tell you my biggest secret,' she said, sitting straighter now, and there was the echo of something lost in her voice. 'I don't want to live, and live, and live forever.'

Her eyes filled with light, hands clasped in a prayer-like mudra, she leant forward and kissed him with intense passion. He prised her hands apart and pulled her towards him until their bodies were locked.

'Nothing should ever be made to do anything against its will,' he said. 'Not even characters in a story.'

She stared into his eyes. 'Especially not characters in a story,' she said, laughing. Then her face seemed to shimmer like moon-struck water. 'You don't really believe that though, do you?

'I don't know... I just don't know any more.' He thought for a while. Her face transfigured, a strange, wild beauty flashed across her features. 'I know you will do something wonderful, Dreamweaver. I know it, and you know it, and you're going there.'

Talis pulled herself free and backed away slightly. She sat watching him, the exaltation on her face clouding over until it was replaced by a sad, heavy look; it was as if an unexplained reason had broken through the stream of feelings and visions.

'You know what they say, Dreamweaver. They say sleep is close to death.' Her fists clenched. 'The dead can walk straight into dreams. They can come back from the void, come alive, and say and do things. They walk out of death as if they were crossing a shallow stream.'

She looked thoughtful. 'I started to think how, if they can find their way back as far as dreams, maybe there's a way back to life – all the way back. I mean, what I'm saying is maybe I'm just dreaming, and this is how I find my way back to life, and you've come here to guide me across the stream and back into life. That's really why you're in this Story.'

Dreamweaver shook his head sadly. 'A beautiful thought,' he said. 'But unfortunately I'm a guide who's more lost than the one he must guide.'

'You're making fun of me now,' she said angrily.

'Talis, this story, this whole thing... '

'I don't understand, Dreamweaver?'

'Look, the Sirens appear on Earth, and they're corrupted by Namida's darkness. So what exactly did manifest on Earth, were they all forms of darkness or were some of them more like Sen?'

'Don't fear the darkness in this Story, Dreamweaver,' she said forcefully. 'It's the ingredient that makes stories flourish, the nourishment. And as for your question, you will need to trace the story, learn it. But I give you my original words...

'a time of wonderment and miracle, but also a time of immeasurable tragedy, desire... and love'

'Now you're avoiding my questions. Look, I'm lying in the wilderness gasping my last fictional breath.'

'That's not my doing,' she snapped. 'Anyway, you don't die this time.'

He was silent for a long while then he said: 'What you said about dreams, walking out of dreams...'

'Yes.'

'Do you think the dead would be foolish enough to cross back into life having once escaped it? In dreams they're free to be dead when they choose without any need for dying.' He studied her. 'If this is a dream, do you think I can walk back into life... well, can I?'

He dropped his gaze. 'I don't think so,' he said wryly.

Talis suddenly came alive, as if reanimated by some mysterious force.

She bit her tongue, her voice drifting off into nothing, like the shadow of a cloud. Then she fell silent, as if the words had somehow fastened her lips.

'Why is my name on the cover of that book, Talis?'

'What book...?'

He looked exasperated. 'Forget it!'

'Please remember my words, Dreamweaver. Your task in this Story is not to look at what can readily be seen, but to find different perspectives. Tell the Story from your own mind, take it into the world with fresh perspective. Make it live again.'

'You've changed it,' he said quickly.

'What do you mean?'

'It was *our* Story – now you are saying, *your* Story. Are we still doing this together?'

'I must leave you now – you're moving away.'

'No wait!'

'I must go....... I.... I.. lo... v'

'Talis!!!!!!'

14

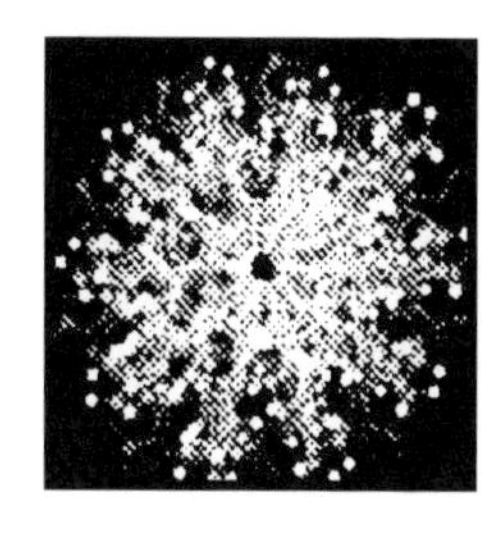

Darkness....... silence....

'Scary isn't it, Dreamweaver? You can't trust anything any more.'

''Who... the..?'

'Oh come, Storyteller, surely I don't have to stand on ceremony.'

'To hell with you, Lynium. You know what, I'm tired of all this.'

'You should have read *The Seed* when you had the chance.' He laughed. 'You know, the bit about how you didn't make it.'

'There seems to be a lot about *me* creeping into this Story, I'm supposed to be learning the script, not playing the lead.'

He thought for a second. 'But you know, I think you want to tell me something, Lynium. I think you've broken away because you can't bear the way you come across in the story. Tell me, what did you do that's so terrible? What are you so ashamed of, and why do you want me out so badly? I mean, it's only a story, I've told millions of them, and they're slowly feeding the collective imagination, bringing it back from the dreamless time.'

'Listen, Storyteller... it's got nothing to do with my ego, let's get that straight. I've told you and you don't get it. If you tell this Story you'll bring such misery into the world... I can't even begin to...'

'Try, Lynium.'

'Damn you, Dreamweaver. I'm getting you out, I'm going to destroy you, destroy you so you'll never even dream again. There's no time or energy for elaborate explanations. I need you out.'

'Then I'll have to look for them myself.'

'What?'

'As you saw before, I've gleaned a few tricks of my own.'

Lynium laughed. 'Oh yes, they've served you well, so well that you're about to die in the scrub. In the old days, I'd have just left you to get your brains sucked out by the Story, but now you know too much, you've made it too far. Now I must destroy you totally, there's no other way, Dreamweaver. You leave me no choice.'

Dreamweaver smiled. 'Then you leave me no choice, either,' he said. 'You forget I'm an old hand at all this floating in darkness. Wait, I can see something, Lynium. Yes, yes, the Circle is showing me what's in your head...I can feel the words moving in my thoughts.'

'I'm warning you, Dreamweaver, don't play with magical words, you don't know what you're doing.'

'Yes, I can taste their syntax bleeding through the darkness...'

'Dreamweaver I'm warning..... Dreamweaver!!!!...... Noooooooooo!!!!!!!!!!!!!!!'

Incredibly strange sounds poured from Dreamweaver's lips – unintelligible – more like threads of hyperbolic plasma – dancing filaments of imagination.

From within the sounds there emerged a towering and beautiful woman with black underwater hair and gleaming turquoise eyes. She was fleshed in a trillion fractal scales that sparkled like mini stars.

The voluptuous super-being began to dance in slow, seductive movements.

Dreamweaver watched in amazement, unsure of what he was creating. His words had a life of their own, travelling up from her belly, through beautiful multi-coloured chakras, eventually reaching her mouth.

She spoke Dreamweaver's words in a vast, arctic voice…

WE TRAVEL BACK IN TIME TO EARTH

THE GODDESS AND SIREN QUEEN SENIDA IS GUARDIAN OF THE GREAT SPIRIT TECHNOLOGY - RULER OF EARTH AND THE ETERNAL REALM OF THE SEED

SUBJECT – PETER LYNIUM – Status: Outlaw on Earth territories

Mental capacity: Genius - Age: unknown - Ex-Immortal

A wicked smile froze across the super-being's lips. TYPE: High-Grade SPIRIT-TECHNOLOGY (DOWNGRADED TO LIVING FLESH)>>>

THE SETTING FOR THIS STORY – TEMPLE OF SPIRIT TECHNOLOGY

Without moving, Senida glided over to a three-dimensional floating screen blossoming with formulas and strange hieroglyphics.

Her whiteless, jet eyes peered into the shifting, living glyphs. Then reaching in through the screen, she extracted the essence of a dark man dressed in skin-tight black. Then with a single stroke of her fine, dream-anointed finger, the man stood before her looking handsome and psychically muscled.

Turning away, she glided effortlessly over to a web of delicate helix patterns, spun from the abdomens of tiny phantom-like figures.

The surrounding space was a blinding, pure white haze with no discernible shape or form.

Suddenly, her image exploded with the platinum shimmer of a myth come alive. The helix-threads knitted into a sensuous, physical presence. Her hair flowed in long, dark binary trails. Her face became a gorgeous mixture of perfect symmetries: a being of dreams and information.

She turned to the dark man-shape. 'Surprisingly, we have many things in common Mr Lynium.'

He stared past her form into the infinite haze. 'With respect, Goddess, what...'

She held up her hand for silence, her black-hole gaze sucking him into her thoughts. 'Yes, it was a pity we were forced to down-grade your Spirit-Code to flesh. I've studied your case with interest and feel there is...' She paused. 'How shall I put it?.... Some potential.'

Reaching up, she encircled her astonishing head with a thin, milky glow, and transformed her face into a serene-looking facsimile, compassion pouring from her now diamond-white eyes.

Lynium glanced up nervously, standing as though he was about to turn and flee.

'You see Mr, Lynium,' she said in a soft honeyed voice. 'The problem I have with most intelligent life, is its inability to be consistent.'

Morphing back into her former ice-maiden countenance, she continued.

'The human race is particularly obstinate in this respect,' she pressed stubbornly. 'All I have done is give humanity what it desired, endless wealth, power and immortality. Then when the desire became a reality, they developed a rather disgusting sentimentality for time and those simpering inadequate bodies they once lived in. So you see, Mr Lynium, that is why the hallowed Spirit Technology has been withdrawn from the general population.'

'A most regrettable transgression, Goddess,' said Lynium, and it was obvious from the tone of his voice that he suddenly felt the hand of some undesirable fate pushing him forward.

'Good,' said Senida, 'I can see that we understand one another.'

Lynium registered a sudden shudder in his newly acquired flesh. What did she want from him? Careful words, heavy with manipulation – that undertone of friendliness, the shared understandings: her manner communicated they were beings of a wider sophisticate who understood matters beyond the current meme.

He edged cautiously. 'Great Goddess, am I to understand that you have something in mind where I am concerned?'

Senida laughed, sending a wave of nausea across the physical world. 'Well, you know Mr Lynium – or may I call you Peter? I like a spirit with spirit. Oh, forgive my…I 'm forgetting you no longer possess a select Spirit-Code.'

Lynium cautioned a nervous laugh. 'Great Goddess, pardon my effrontery, but am I to know what you have planned for me?'

Senida focused down on Lynium, her eyes flashed licentiously like tiny, imploding stars. Lynium's whole being screamed, no resonance escaped. He was afraid to speak, fearful that his voice might betray him. The aura of a terrible prospect surrounded him, and the gaping mouth of eternity opened up, ready to swallow.

He managed an acrid smile. 'Great goddess, I ask if…'

'Silence,' ordered Senida. 'You forget yourself, Peter. Remember I can see inside the minds of *men*, and can enervate anything which courts my displeasure.'

'Ye… yes, of course, Great Goddess,' stammered Lynium.

'Let me explain,' she said. 'I have decided that it is time for me to become better aquainted with something derived from the frail human condition… on a more… intimate level. It is felt that a coupling of this nature will assist myself and the Sirens in the delicate apparatus of government by offering the misery of humanity a hybrid being, half flesh, half Spirit-Code.' She smiled frighteningly. 'My first response to this matter was to simply trance a zygote from one of the species, however, my dark vespertine has developed a certain fascination for the base act of coitus.'

She moved forward…

Lynium glaciered……. He closed his eyes. 'And the outcome?' he asked, drained of emotion.

She weighed his question, and there was something inevitable and terrifying in her reply.

'I shall bestow the vestment of prescience upon this prodigy,' she offered casually, as though this was a common, every day occurrence. 'He will essentially be the link: the one who delivers me to the people to be worshiped. The subjugator. He will roil in the grimed sludge of flesh and gestate in the symbiosis of my Technology with equal validity.' She suddenly let out a hideous, vestigial laugh. 'And of course I will ensure that he suffers horribly, just to give him the appropriate messiah branding.'

'Need I ask, why me?' questioned Lynium hopelessly.

She sighed. 'Oh, I think you know, don't you, Peter. You have a … how shall I put it… a certain reputation in the Spirit World.' Then she added: 'And perhaps most importantly, you have no compassion for anything, not even yourself.'

She stopped and stared straight into his eyes. 'Peter.'

Eternity seemed to pass before his eyes like a flow of solid information.

Corpse-pale, Senida smiled a blinding flash of melting anti-matter, her eyes glowing like suns eclipsed. Lynium's eyes flicked back into his head. In his mind he conjured a face, delicate and fine, skin tanned and translucent, a block of alabaster lit from within. Then his thoughts were invaded. Now the features contained elements of not one, but many women, beautiful and repulsive. The exquisite sensuality of a youth in full blossom – fertile and abundant with time (destroyed) – the tended geometry of a radiant adult (destroyed) – the senility of extreme age drifting close to death (destroyed)…

This pungent synthesis scorched across his mind.

Then he heard a woman singing to him in some intricate foreign tongue. The tones brushed against his body with invisible fingers. These fingers were working around his abdomen and groin. They were cool and stimulating, expert and precise. He grew into their grasp. He'd never experienced such fervent experiment, manipulated by waves of soft rhythm to the point of abandon, then back down to begin the process afresh. The caress grew more forceful, he started to gasp and then scream; on it went unrelenting… more… more… more..

His eyes flicked open. And he wished they hadn't>>>>>

He watched in horror as an evil dark fog poured from Senida's sex. It seemed to be bulging up and around her in the shape of a demon wrapped in her gaseous technologies. He began to convulse in violent spasms. With a snatching motion the demon-thing lifted his milky skin like a sheet of fine silk, then gripping a handful of veins and arteries it tore them free and sculpted the tangled mass onto its own nitrous integument.

The Senida-demon moved her hands slowly and lasciviously across Lynium's deconstructed body. With an expression of appalling relish she drew him to a close, and he emptied into a chasm so vast it swallowed his mind.

Her eyes rolled back….. lips licking…..

For a second Senida allowed her victim to become fully cognisant. This was no act of mercy, but a cruel twist so she could witness every micro-second of his dissolution.

Lynium's desperate eyes opened and fixed on his exo-lover. The terrible realisation that dawned upon him at that moment simply heightened Senida's pleasure. Together they'd composed an anthem of pain and misery. Lynium felt the touch of Senida flow into him like a living torrent of darkness and her mouth brushed against his mouth, an exposed wound calling for platelets.

The moment was cauterised and everything became a frozen slick, without ambition…….. a muffled shock wave. A caustic vision pulsing across two realities.

The dissolution becomes the union.

The unlived transmutes its essence.

"AHHHHHHHHHHHHHHHHHHHHHHHHHHHHHH"…Lynium screamed himself into oblivion…..

15

Dreamweaver opened his eyes. He peered into a vast gauzy blueness.

His senses arrived on the next wave of thoughts as thin clouds smeared the canvas. Then came another and another until the blue became splashed with ochre. The clouds rubbed their vaporous bodies through sandy pleats whilst the sky pounded with courtship rhythms. Crash, crash... then a blinding sheet of light...

He painfully sat up, brushing the scrub's ashy vestment from his body. The clouds soon fled from the heat's liquefied shimmer as the sun claimed its place at the head of the sky. His mouth had been invaded in the night, and he spat out a round of spittle-basted cadavers into the sand. *Hardly a fitting breakfast*, he thought.

His head pounded like a runner's heart, and his face was like an ancient papyrus. But still he found the strength to drag himself up. Several of his bones threatened to pierce through great patches of sand-blasted skin on his shoulders and knees. The wind had scrubbed him clean, wiped him blank of detail, and made him less attached to his cells.

The scrub had greater things in store though. Once he'd lifted himself, he almost collapsed back into the sand with shock.

Directly beside him was a thin, pre-natal mound threatening to deliver a body into the sunlight. Without thinking, Dreamweaver moved towards what logic told him was the head, and began scraping the ashen swaddling. The calcified granules came away to reveal a pair of eyes welded shut by tear-moistened silica.

The eyes cracked open…

Dreamweaver jerked back. 'Lynium,' he said venomously. 'Lynium.'

Lynium slowly rose from his soft sarcophagus and fixed his gaze on Dreamweaver. His dark, semi-automatic features displayed their journey, looking collapsed and sickly against their powdery frame.

A cavalcade of tiny cockroaches poured from his lips like crawling saliva, and he spat them out without shifting his gaze for a second. It was now, as his clothes hung in tatters that Dreamweaver saw how Lynium's body was made almost entirely of elaborate prosthetics. There were several large gashes across the fleshy armature of his arms which oozed a lurid green liquid that smelt sickly-sweet. His legs and abdominal parts boasted a flickering perversion of movements that formed the exotic meat of his falsehood. The illusion of biology was shattered.

'Yes,' said Lynium, 'take a good look, Storyteller, take a good look. I warned you not to play that sequence. I warned you!!!'

Dreamweaver stood and looked down on the damaged machine-man.

'I'm sorry, Lynium,' he said. 'I had no…'

'Save it,' snapped Lynium in a harsh, metallic voice. 'Now it ends.'

He had no time to waste on nostalgia; he was on the verge of extinction with oblivion hovering at his lips like a lover's kiss. His dust-framed eyes were bright with focused awareness.

Lifting his arm, a seething clump of glistening metal morphed through his fingers as if its potential was somehow embedded in his hand. As he aimed it at Dreamweaver's head it solidified into a clumsy approximation of a pistol.

Dreamweaver closed his eyes. *Enough is enough*, he thought.

Lynium's cyborg finger gently squeezed the pistol's malformed trigger.

The wind blew… Heat gelled the hills… lizards lammed their prey…

A universe of heartbeats...

'Damn you, Storyteller, damn you to hell and back.'

Dreamweaver opened his eyes gently. 'Finish it, Lynium,' he said coldly, 'You were right all along. I can't make it. I can't change the Story.'

'I don't know what to think!' said Lynium in a roughened, aged voice.

Then, abruptly, he relaxed. He lowered his arm as the pistol imploded back into his fingers. 'Listen, Storyteller, and listen well,' he said slowly.

These words were a vision echoed in Dreamweaver's ears. They moved through him with solid precision. 'I'm listening,' he said calmly.

'Look past me and tell me what you see,' said Lynium.

Dreamweaver did as he was asked; then a smile broke across his face. 'The Circle,' he said. 'I must have carved a huge circle myself.'

Lynium flinched in pain. 'Get me over to the Circle,' he said, 'and make it quick.'

Dreamweaver knelt down and helped Lynium sit up properly, brushing the remainder of the sand from his face and lips. His body was damaged and degraded. He had no way of knowing how to stem the secretions from Lynium's prosthetics.

'These look pretty bad,' he said.

Lynium seemed unconcerned. 'Just get me over to the Circle, for God's sake,' he barked.

'Something wrong with my bedside manner?' remarked Dreamweaver tartly. 'And I hope you're not going to disappear on me just when it starts getting interesting.'

'OK, funny man,' said Lynium.

Dreamweaver moved behind Lynium and heaved him onto his feet. 'There,' he said. 'How do you feel about moving?'

Lynium let out a deep moan. 'I feel lousy about everything,' he said. 'And what have you lost this time?'

'Lost?'

'Damn you, Storyteller, you must start paying attention if you're going to make it out of this alive and save your infernal world.... The book, idiot, the damn book you dropped in the sand.' He let out a deep sigh. 'Hhhhhhaaarrr, so I'm supposed to do everything for you?'

Dreamweaver looked around helplessly. 'I can't see it.'

Lynium pointed, and without warning, an even cruder pistol melded from his hand. 'Damn,' he growled, shaking it back inside. He pointed again. 'There, over there...'

Dreamweaver moved over to a small mound of sand and exhumed the book. He was just about to place it in his pocket, when he noticed that the cover had changed. It now displayed a picture of Senida flanked by her army of Sirens. He looked anxiously at Lynium, but before the words passed his lips the outlaw said:

'It's changed, hasn't it?'

'Yes.'

'Senida?'

'Yes.'

'That's not a good sign,' offered Lynium. 'Not good at all.'

The stark light illuminated beads of perspiration on his forehead. He seemed an odd creature, as though nature had spawned something unsure of its purpose. There was still an unquestionable humanity beneath the profusion of synthetics, and also a strength of will that heightened his mortal condition.

Lynium's origin remained an enigma, yet by twenty-five, he was the world's most gifted physicist, and also its most prolific outlaw. He possessed a brilliant conceptual mind and an insatiable appetite for adventure. His fascination with Spirit Technology had taken him to the threshold of destruction on numerous occasions. But somehow, he'd always found methods to stealth his Spirit-Code back into The Seed. That is, until his most renowned escapade went horribly wrong.

Following an aborted attempt to infiltrate Senida's Sacred Lexicon, to steal the secrets of Spirit Technology, he was stripped of all levels of Spirit-Code. He was thus confined to the suffering understudy of corporeal existence, the transcendent umbilical snipped and tucked.

He had never been interested in joining the fettered Spirits coursing The Seed. How could entities that had grown tired of long and sunny days cope with the concept of existence without ending?

His motives were different. He had plans for his own version of eternity and was prepared to take very serious risks to achieve his objective. There was a distinct ritualistic quality to his plans, which made his small cognoscenti grow dreamy at Spirit Technology.

In Lynium they saw an existence that was a revenge upon the painless sorrow of a heaven that failed to spellbind despite its miraculous interface. The elaborate crimes that flowed through his mind were the most daring ever attempted: they had challenged the supremacy of Senida and her Sirens.

Peter Lynium understood that this leviathan act of defiance against Senida would make it impossible for him to ever drift in the gossamer realm of The Seed again: that is, without the most skillful of all deceptions. This thought had brought him no sadness.

Upon reaching the Circle, Lynium let go of Dreamweaver and plunged himself into its decorative features. He bathed in the static as if it were the soundness of a healing spa. He splashed it about his body in rich, loamy clods of information, then climbed out, walking across its surface like walking on a painted lake. In the process, the liquefied rebus had somehow knitted his damaged prostheses, and his tattered clothes looked pristined by a virtual tailor.

He gestured lazily from the centre of the Circle. 'Come on,' he shouted. 'It will make you feel better.'

Dreamweaver hesitated. 'This had better not be one of your tricks, Lynium,' he warned.

A scowl bled across Lynium's nitrous features. 'Senseless,' he said. 'Now that's really senseless, Storyteller, I could have blown your brains out back there, but no, instead I decide to drown you in static.' He let out a sarcastic laugh. 'That's the kind of insane thing you'd do isn't it Story-man. Now shut up and get in, we've got a lot of work to get through if you're going to save the world... God help them,' he added sarcastically

Reluctantly, Dreamweaver edged himself into the Circle, and was surprised to find it warm and spumy with a pleasant scent. He doused his tired body, feeling invigorated by the mysterious non-fluid.

Lynium sat on the edge of the Circle and glared in silence, the way a predator assesses its prey. His jet-black hair blew across his face, and in the slanting light he took on the appearance of a carbonised banraku. He looked incapable of absorbing a single ray of light, a single spark of hope.

When they had finished their remaking, the two men sat together on the Circle's edge. Lynium had used his clumpy pistol-hand to kill a large lizard as it languished in the last rays of sunlight. Then he'd morphed his stumpy appendage into a flourishing cluster of flames to roast the catch.

As the strange incarnation that was Lynium began to torch the meat, Dreamweaver thought of Talis, and the small clearing where they had touched in a dream; it seemed as if it had happened to someone else and years had passed. He thought how so often in his stories, lovers had been doomed to never touch, and how when they died alone on a battlefield, pinned through the heart, there was scarcely a trickle from the death-wound. Their faces were ashen and smiling as life departed.

In his mind he suddenly saw Talis. Her eyes as she lifted them, grew wide and dreamy. Still in his mind's eye he looked up, and in the fading depths of the sky, a ghostly smile of a new moon had appeared. Her voice called out to him like a thick sheet of moonlight, '*Help me, Dreamweaver, help me, Dreamweaver.*' He was shaking and he couldn't tell if it was horror or desire... again she called in a rush of lume,

'Dreamweaver, the evil Goddess knows I've fallen in love with you…'

In Dreamweaver's mind – a shimmering silver ghost of information depicted Talis fashioned with elaborate sex and veiled with intricate weapons standing in a glistening forest.

Alien females dripping with animal dreams surrounded her. Slowly, in turn, she annihilated each alien with shameless pleasure, releasing the animal dreams into the forest to roam amongst the ancient shrubs.

A glimpse through the trees revealed a luscious, green valley. She made her way to its feminine slopes dispatching more assailants as she went. Then, she studied her magical surroundings. Realising how disconnected and removed she felt, disposessed of the starlit realm of creation, she was suddenly compelled to impose all the damage at her disposal upon the sun, the clouds, the succulent Earth and all the life that it yielded.

A radiant Senida walked from the shameless pleasure of darkness, and this time Talis lowered her defences and drank in her presence like a dazzling yearning.

She touched Senida like a ghost-lover then turned sharply and glared at Dreamweaver.

"You fool,' she laughed. "They always said you were going nowhere. Now nowhere is coming to you. You will end up a piece of fiction, addiction – dereliction."

Talis licked at Senida's mouth, and then she turned to Dreamweaver.

"Knowing beneath what is written, you'll always be twice bitten, twice in the wrong place, twice in the wrong time."

She laughed like a hyena….

'The story will try and get rid of you now,' said Lynium, handing Dreamweaver a piece of waxy meat. 'Now that I've decided to help you.'

Jerked back from his thoughts, Dreamweaver stared at him for a long time. 'I know she's in trouble,' he finally offered in a low voice. 'You saw that too?'

'Probably not in the same way as you… but, yes I saw it.'

'Listen,' insisted Lynium. 'Don't be fooled by the what you see in this Circle, it's just the same fabric as dreams… nothing more.'

'I don't understand.'

'No.'

'Look, eat your food, it's geting cold. I'll put you in the picture. If you're going to survive, you'll need a few facts about this Story that you were never meant to know.'

Lynium tore a greedy lump of meat away from a bone. 'Firstly, let's go over that nasty little episode about me that you dragged out of the darkness.'

Dreamweaver went to speak. '…'

'Shut up, Storyteller,' growled Lynium. 'Save your stupid questions until I've finished. Let's get one thing straight: I don't give a damn about you, and I didn't spare your inimical presence just for you to go on an ego trip with that girl. Clear?'

Dreamweaver smiled at Lynium's rudeness. 'Do you treat everyone with such contempt?' he asked calmly.

Lynium cast an impatient glance at Dreamweaver. 'Now,' he continued. 'As I was saying, that nasty little episode with Senida. Well, that was the catalyst of this whole Story, and in fact, it was your ability to summon it from the depths of the Story and speak it as you did that saved your worthless life.'

Dreamweaver nodded thoughtfully.

'Until then,' continued Lynium. 'I had you branded a loser in my book – and in this book too,' he added spitefully. 'But you have now demonstrated that you truly possess the strength of transcendence; the strength to consciously cross the boundaries between fact and fiction, reality and hyper reality. I knew the Storytellers could dream, but I just couldn't take the chance, and especially not with someone as careless and clumsy as you.'

He touched his chin thoughtfully. 'There's a second reason why you're still here,' he said coldly. 'In summoning the vision, you effectively destroyed me… come on, don't look so shocked, there's no time for worthless gestures.'

Lynium glared angrily. 'My cover's blown, compromised beyond repair… meaning I'm finished in this Story. Worse still,' he moaned, 'is the nauseating reality that you're now the only one who has any chance of saving the world from the intolerable misery heading its way.'

Dreamweaver felt a surge of fear rise and twist his thoughts. *No*, he thought, *why me?*

'Yeah!' said Lynium. 'My thought exactly, but that's it, we're stuck with it now, so we'd better try and make the best of… ' He tore off another chunk of meat and sat chewing.

Dreamweaver followed suit, and to his surprise, it tasted exactly like the fruit from the upside-down tree.

Lynium looked at him. 'Yes, I know. This Story is not good when it comes to taste. It's big on visuals, but taste, forget it!' He tossed another bone into the Circle and watched it disappear into the roils of static.

'Anyway… all very interesting,' he said. 'But I digress. Now, let's get to the heart of it all. You've got most of the Story up to here: Namida, then all that fiasco with Sen, then the big showdown that sent that little bundle of joy out into space. Finally you saw how the damned thing ended up on Earth and hatched out this monster we know as Senida.' He smiled. 'Nice, ironic little touch, Sen-ida…'

Dreamweaver stared at him impassively.

Lynium's eyes flashed. 'OK… now this is where the whole thing turns on its head. In the 'healing' nonsense that Talis was going to feed you, it all pans out in the standard format. That's to say, the evil Goddess Senida turns up on nice, little Earth, spreads misery and violence across the entire planet, constructs this miracle-soaked realm –The Seed – where all her cronies can prance through eternity, destroying and dreaming up new types of evil.'

He cast a dreamy smile at Dreamweaver. 'Then, as if touched by some omnipotent hand, Senida discovers the part of herself that is Sen, the Goddess of healing. Zing...! Everything is transformed. The world is healed of all its suffering, she brings all those poor bastards she slaughtered back to life and cleanses all traces of malevolence from The Seed.

Lynium looked up and smiled as though an angel had touched his soul. 'Uh...... ha' he sighed blissfully. 'And the Earth flourished under the miracle-spun hands of Senida. Talis would have put it more eloquently, but then she is beautifully designed to tell stories to people in your line of business. And, how brilliant her words sound, don't you think, so rich in narrative, the delicious embellishments, so uplifting?' He lowered his gaze. 'Remember way back in the beginning, how magical, how super-sensed it all felt.'

His head flicked up in a sudden movement. 'And remember how Talis gave it all that little edge, remember...*"in the visions you've gazed upon a time lost in the Earth's memory, a time of wonderment and miracle, but also a time of immeasurable tragedy, desire... and love"*. Lynium smiled. 'Nice the way she dropped in the "Love",' he said.

'And of course followed with... *"As we go deeper into the Story, we'll be moving to stranger and more distant places, realms of immeasurable chaos. It's important to know that in these places I cannot guide you. You must find your own methods to gather the Story."*... Now that was a great little touch,' he said almost joyfully. 'The clever detailing, the way she made it real for you, the way it all seemed as though you'd find your own unique way through the chaos. The brave Dreamweaver, who emerges holding the Story, golden in his hands. Oh yes, she'd subject you to a few horrors, a few close scrapes, but all cleverly orchestrated.

'Ah! I nearly forgot, all the "I don't know what I am" retoric, all those layers of vulnerability. Very convincing, don't you think?'

Dreamweaver looked very serious. *The more you feel like you belong, the less you must belong*, he thought to himself. 'Carry on,' he said calmly. 'Let's not break the flow.'

Lynium nodded. 'In her velvet trance-tones she would have explained how a great renaissance in scholarly matters and radical art blossomed from every corner of the globe. How Senida's loving image was fashioned from shimmering alien substances, which glinted and moved to invisible rhythms. And how children danced, and old men and women sat contentedly beside vast maps of The Seed and studied peacefully, safe in the knowledge that deterioration and death were quenched. If that was what they wished of course, yes, all very respectful, creative and peaceful.'

He sighed again. 'Uh...... and here comes the jewel-in-the-crown,' he said softly. 'Dreamweaver returns to his troubled, dreamless world and tells them this wondrous story,'

Lynium lifted his arms in a gesture of blissful surrender. 'Ahh... and when all of the people have finished drying their wonder-filled eyes, still more unfolds. By telling this beautiful story, the handsome and brave Dreamweaver breaks the mysterious spell of the Circle; it opens its vaporous symmetries and out floats Senida clasping the power of dreams in her outstretched arms...AS SHE IS NOW!!!!!...' screamed, Lynium, showering Dreamweaver with spittle and unchewed lizard. 'Oh, God,' he moaned, 'as she is... sacred and evil.'

Dreamweaver jerked back abruptly. Then he moved to touch Lynium's arm. 'Look, Lynium...'

'Save it,' snapped Lynium. 'We haven't yet touched her miracle-soaked explanation of how this vast lachrymose became entombed in a circle...a circle.'

Lynium fell silent, his gaze fixed ahead.

Dreamweaver sensed with hyper-clarity that his fate was now entwined with all fellow beings. That this was no longer a sinister contrivance with no other price but the loss of his own being. *Very well,* he thought, *I must summon all my strength and focus every storytelling skill I possess to resolve this.* His eyes narrowed with new determination as his soul grew steady and focused.

A deep russet tinged the landscape. Small, fat clouds dipped their bellies on the horizon like giants floating in a great, rusty sea. The wind had started to pick up again and the air was full of flies attracted by the lizard meat. Energy streamed through Dreamweaver's body wrapping itself around his heart. It jabbed. It jabbed.

He turned to face Lynium, head on. 'OK, Lynium, now you can take something from me,' he said forcefully. 'I don't like you – and if I had any other choice I'd never trust you further than I could throw you, which narrows it down fine for me.' His eyes burned through Lynium's face. 'Now, we're going to finish this without any more expletives or embellishments from you. If you want to see this finished then spare me the drama.'

Dreamweaver held the tension. 'Now move to your version. I want to know exactly why the coupling of you and Senida turns this ship around. So get on with it!'

Lynium scowled from deep behind his eyes. Then he nodded. 'Sure, Storyteller, sure,' he said gently.

He continued. 'It goes like this, Storyteller. Senida used me in mortal form to fertilise her Spirit-zygote, which is when I picked up these injuries.' He flinched as though the memory was caustic.

Dreamweaver nodded in silence.

'Anyway, as you saw in graphic detail, she had plans for this unfortunate offspring,' continued Lynium.

'I, of course, had none,' he added shakily. 'This pulsing life-spark lay fully cognisant inside Senida's dark, dreamy womb, and conceived its own prescient mind structure before it had even become a foetus. It was in effect an adept in mind-science and transcendent technologies… It had already seen and accepted its own destructive fate within the oracular flow of creation. However, at some point during the gestation, this hybrid persona experienced the blissful touch of something made from pure, untarnished consciousness. In other words, it met the healing essence of Sen, which lay dormant inside Senida. This beloved synthesis remained charged with logic-defying potential, whilst cleverly screening its union from Senida's sharp, psychic insight.'

Lynium smiled and his joyless features suddenly ignited. 'When the child was born, it took the corporeal appearance of a human man, yet every eye that feasted on this sacriscious image was granted its own unique experience of this man-form – nothing was fixed'

'The Seed Singer,' said Dreamweaver slowly. 'The Seed Singer.'

Lynium nodded and gestured towards Dreamweaver's left pocket. 'The book,' he said, 'Please take out the book.... good, now think of what I have just said and let it fall open.'

Dreamweaver looked down at the words spread out across the pages.

~ E A R T H D R E A M S ~

Book of Wisdom – Lexicon of The Seed Singer.

The Seed Singer was unique. As he spun his words, there came a point where the words were speaking us into existence; and we became their mystic forms, not their receptor. Often his words vibrated like the movements of a new type of consciousness. We would listen to his wisdom feeding its blissful thread through the labyrinth of our minds.

Within his words there were areas of surface abstract, moving unexplained, anarchic and fevered; where the entire structure of his voice was undefined, explosive and exalted.

From this mesmerising state The Seed Singer transformed us. We saw him stripping away the evil of Spirit Technology.

At first, his image came to us like drafts of dreaming air. His body was of every conceivable human. His arms were snake-like branches of love: this gift from The Seed ran over our skin like insects fed with bliss. All parts of us became entwined in his body.

His eyes encircled our entire spectrum like transparent angels, their wings growing and crumbling in constant showers of feeling. Once implanted, he worked it so that he energised the soul of each person.

The voice remained constant, sending out his wisdom in deep soothing tones. Everywhere one travelled all you could hear was pure Seed Singer pulsing through psychic platforms.

The Seed Singer gave wondrous questions to our answers and life to our meaning.

'The words in the book are all I have of him,' said Lynium sadly, 'his image has been meticulously erased from the Story.'

'Tell me what happened?' demanded Dreamweaver.

Lynium frowned as if a dark cloud had just drifted across the brightness of his mind's eye. 'To begin with, The Seed Singer did not court Senida's displeasure,' he said in a slow, unsteady voice. 'She was preoccupied with developing a new type of evil Spirit-Witch, and was quite content to let him walk amongst the mortals, witnessing the sadness of time and entropy. But the people loved him and he bathed them in a lustrous compassion, the likes of which they had never felt. Despite the pain I suffered at his conception, I was honoured to have played some hand in the making of this beautiful being. He would come to me and speak with the humility of a son who loves and respects his father.'

The frown deepened. 'Then, as if ignited by some glorious flame, The Seed Singer set about disengaging his prescience from the evil that Senida had hidden within its fate. You see he understood perfectly the mechanisms of Ethereal Technologies, he could weave new threads from Senida's ugly tangle. But the one thing he could not untangle was his own suffering. This was indelibly scribed on the parchment of time, and he made no attempt to reverse this composition.'

Tears were now pouring from Lynium's time-bitten eyes. He gestured for Dreamweaver to use the book again. 'Open it, open it!'

'I get the feeling this is it,' said Dreamweaver. 'This is where I find out what this is all about.'

Lynium nodded. 'It's time, Dreamweaver. Open it.'

Dreamweaver held the book shut, then gently let it flop open. Then he looked.

~ E A R T H D R E A M S ~

Book of Wisdom – Destruction of The Seed Singer.

Clouds dissolved from a thunderous sky, exposing a hell-red sun, and the light it shed upon the streets, merged with the blood and ruin. Many people had become frenzied tearing one another apart limb from limb, then slashing dead bodies with anything to hand. Heads were severed and carried by children like playground trophies. Dogs turned on their owners and screamed obscenities in loud human voices – no fear of retribution, no sanctity of life.

This was the scene as the Sirens came to take The Seed Singer back to Senida. They swooped down through the conflagration, down, down, down from the eternal realm of The Seed.

The Seed Singer, bathed in a milky glow, looked out on the torture these creatures had spread, and for the first time he truly knew sadness for the plight of mortals. Then, as if atoms were like clay in his hands, he reshaped the destruction into beauty and order, and the people awoke from a dark slumber to find their bodies and minds effused with his love.

Suddenly, the Sirens were upon him, having tracked The Seed Singer through portable black holes. They had pure white faces with screaming spirits for eyes.

'Seed Singer,' screamed one of them. 'Your Mother has sent us to bring you home.'

The Seed Singer smiled. 'Tell her I've relocated.'

The Sirens laughed hysterically and turned on the crowd. A gasp of utter terror rippled through every person. The Seed Singer simply waved his arm sending a gleaming arc of light across the entire crowd. Tears fell from peoples' eyes as they now saw what he would sacrifice to preserve their lives. Their protector had taken the unique energy needed for this action from his own aura, exposing himself to the rampant atrocities stored within the Sirens.

Seeing that their action to destroy the crowd was blocked, one of the Sirens tossed her gleaming black hair until it transformed into strange and spiteful weapons.

She cried out: 'Look what a fool this Seed Singer is, look how he's laid himself bare to save these miserable mortals.' And with that she flung her spite at The Seed Singer. Her weapons, crawling thick with hate and vengeance, left their mark on his radiant body, but miraculously didn't wound him.

The Seed Singer moved forward in the trough that time had dug for him. He had seen these images a trillion times etched in the psyche of his prescience, and now he walked in pace with their allotted space in time.

'I am the blazing light,' he said, and his eyes glistened like liquid fire. 'It is the shadow that follows and bathes in my glory. So down you go and bathe, Shadow.'

This drove the Sirens wild with rage. Pointing her finger, a second Siren conjured up an angry ball of pain from her dreaming biology and hurled it at The Seed Singer, but even as it flew through the air he spoke it down with soft, healing words.

'Look into my eyes, Pain, you will fall harmless at my feet.'

The pain fell at his feet as if humbled, asking for forgiveness for having orchestrated such a terrible assault.

The Sirens grew furious and launched the most massive attack, increasing in violence until all restraint was lost and manic fury rained down upon The Seed Singer. Their weapons were almost rendered useless by the skill of his maverick words, had the Sirens not screamed backwards re-mixing his beautiful sounds so that at last their clumps of pain grew crimson with his spiritual blood.

It was then that Senida melted through the fabric of time and stood before her damaged son. She was an image of darkness, a lightning-shadow of unimaginable beauty, bereft of physics.

Great swathes of people let out a mournful cry and bowed their heads to avoid her toxic gaze. She was here to claim her son from the clutches of her clone Sisters.

Crowds gathered under The Seed Singer's glowing shield and began to sing. The atmosphere was thick with love for this beautiful being.

Senida's eyes filled with soft, silver light and corpse-cold flames invaded her flesh. Her hair shone with an evil, seeing lustre.

'It is time to come home my son,' she said calmly. 'You have disappointed me greatly by diverging from the fate that I had conceived for you.'

The Seed Singer smiled back knowingly. 'Then I must find a way to continue this trend.'

Senida stayed calm and rational. 'You have the gift to distinguish every shape and path that you have not yet placed your foot upon. You claim to see what your Spirit-Code will encounter in flesh: every passage of every complex nook,' she said. 'But somehow you cannot see the problem with the path you are choosing.'

'I see it,' he said, 'I see that it is now time for you to give me your gift.'

'Your prescience is misguided, there is no gift for you.'

He smiled. 'It has not let me down, Mother.'

'How is that?' questioned Senida.

'No time for questions, I must claim my gift,' replied The Seed Singer.

Rage suddenly ignited Senida's face. 'An end to this episode!!!!' she screamed, as she unleashed all her rage on The Seed Singer. It took a pico-second for the damage to register on his already weakened body. His face was not shocked, enraged or horrified in the slightest. He was at peace with the hand of fate.

He made no attempt to activate his advanced Spirit-Code, and so avoid the wrenching pain. He looked as if a bomb had ripped him apart, the front of his body was a squelching mass of crimson.

His eyes remained fixed on Senida, and his smile refused to fade. Blood gushed through his lips as though he had just drank from a sacrificial calf.

Senida towered over him. 'You were a regrettable experiment,' she bellowed. 'But now it is over,'

He looked up. 'Yes it is over,' he said. 'And you have at last delivered your great gift to me.' He sagged onto the floor.

Senida hovered nervously, seemingly transfixed by his shattered presence. 'Gift!!!!' she screamed, 'Gift!!!! There is no gift, only pain, endless pain.'

The Seed Singer nodded gently. 'Yes,' he said. 'Yeeeees. The pain will be the mantra that keeps my focus. Pain is the gift housed in my flesh, and you have delivered it to me.' He took a shuddering breath and slowly closed his eyes. His supervene mind reached into the timeless singularity to deliver his final resplendent act of will and love. Thus he dragged the entire Story back into the emptiness from which all things emerge: the meaningless point where vast realms rest as miniscule threads of pure possibility.

Every thought, every microfilament of experience, every pain, every memory, from the instant Senida fell to Earth, was hauled from its vibrational mooring. Great swathes of imagination flashed across The Seed Singer's awareness: a spectrum of endless dimensions, plucked from the mind of God. He saw every misery the Sirens had inflicted, understood their thoughts in kaleidoscopic detail. Cocooned in The Seed Singer's mind lay this whole Story: a larva of violence and unhappiness that must never be allowed to escape. But tethered like a mule to the Sirens and their monstrous realm of The Seed, went the power of human dreams and all the wonders it contained; in this the Seed Singer had no choice.

The Universe faltered as Earth jumped with the kick of a circuit breaking. Reality desperately tried to fill the gap as two separate Times fused together. People collided with long-dead relatives, as they in turn met a future not meant for their eyes. Conscious machines examined their plodding ancestors; everything was confused. Then the quantum field renewed the business of life… it carried on… devoid of dream power… it carried on…

Senida's after-glow burned into the void like a psychic supernova. Understanding of her condition washed through her in a wave of mutilated memories. For every instant of evil, there now existed countless projections, things fated but unable to become. An invisible self within her enciphered this as her will, but it had no power to manifest. *Strange*, she thought, *I still understand it is possible though.* Yet for all these miracles, the plucked time hovered unsteadily in its new home, held only by the trance-lock of The Seed Singer. Dimensional reality would not give up its children willingly and demanded that some trace, no matter how small be left behind. The Seed Singer willed it as small as possible, so that a point no larger than a pinhead was placed upon Earth to act as the counterbalance.

As time didn't pass, Senida's disenfranchisement understood more of its predicament. It found methods to operate as wisps of possibility within the silent ambience, closing around The Seed Singer's holding force.

Assessing there was no possible chance of synthesis; it set about eroding the force, groping ingeniously until it found to its delight the strength it needed encased within.

In a hidden place on Earth the tiny dot began to grow, ever so slowly, pushing its boundaries outward. Possibility was stretching its contiguous void towards probability. Now Senida began to recognise fragmentary instances of her lost awareness, she grew... she grew.... sending out feelers into the world...

16

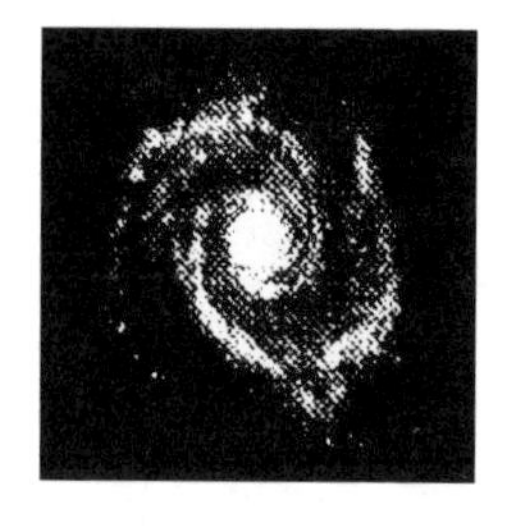

Dreamweaver let the book drop from his fingers, watching it fall in strange, gluey slow motion. An irascible wasteland stretched out before him, a beast ready to devour him. Fear lay quivering in his belly, wet and saturated with too many unanswered questions. The scrub punched him with its wind, it was dark and monstrous, a place of emptiness and storm-trodden vistas. He contemplated his madness in having imagined that he would succeed and make it through this Story, this radiant myth made out of violence and shadow.

It took some time to gather himself. He stared across at Lynium, slowly squeezing his thoughts together. The two men balanced on the edge of thought until Dreamweaver finally broke the tension.

'So at last, this Story yields the secret of our lost Dream Power,' he said flatly, his face ashen. 'But in the moment of understanding I find myself hovering on the edge of an even greater abyss.' He smiled knowingly. 'Understanding brings no pleasure, however to know that our Great Loss was cast because of such an act of love and sacrifice is...'

He stopped without finishing the sentence. Then said softly: 'I'm truly sorry, Lynium.'

Lynium nodded. 'The Seed Singer recognised that Senida would never be content just enslaving Earth, so he had no other choice. He was wise enough to trust that Nature would find a way to restore Herself; the Storytellers are Her answer.'

'What a poisonous twist,' offered Dreamweaver. 'Those sent to restore humanity will instigate its final destruction.'

'The chilling beauty of Senida's mind,' said Lynium.

Dreamweaver's eyes flashed. 'I need to clarify a few things before we go any further.'

'Make it fast,' said Lynium, 'there's not much time, Storyteller. Senida will have plucked the vision you summoned and know I'm active. She will know I've shown you the truth and will stop at nothing to destroy us now; she has no choice.'

'But how does my part in this work. I still don't understand how my telling the Story will release Senida from the Circle?'

'It's complex, with no time for a lesson in physics,' said Lynium, his mind sifting for thoughts. 'Basically, it centres on the concepts of possibility and probability. The more strings that emanate from a possibility stored in the void, the more probable its manifestation becomes. Thought in its purest form attracts possibility like a magnet. It is therefore the hand that pulls the strings into being. Essentially, each individual shapes the reality they experience through the thoughts they send out. And on a greater scale the Collective creates its own experience again.'

'So what you're saying is that by telling this Story and spreading it into the Collective Consciousness, there are going to be countless hands pulling on strings. The people will literally give the Story reality.'

'Precisely,' said Lynium. 'But we have to remember that in this case we're not dealing with just an ordinary bunch of possibilities and probabilities. These are events that have already happened, so without the force of The Seed Singer they would never be allowed back into the void. The whole thing is very unstable, very unstable. Enough minds sending out "Senida" thoughts will put intolerable strain on The Seed Singer, eventually sucking the whole miserable saga back into what we may call normal reality.'

'I get the picture,' said Dreamweaver. 'But that still doesn't explain why Senida...Talis...have tried to deceive me with the 'Healing' version as you put it?'

'Oh come on,' groaned Lynium. 'Would you go out there willingly to recount this nightmare to your already sickened world? Besides, the 'Healing' version is perfect. It's the mythic tale of the hero's quest with a happy ending, what could be better? Even more people will send it their thoughts.'

'Yes... yes... yes,' countered Dreamweaver. 'You say that, but the version I'm supposed to tell never happend. Surely then, those thoughts will give rise to a new reality?'

'Oh, for God's sake!' Screamed Lynium. 'They say you're supposed to have a sharp mind, filled with wonders,' he added caustically. 'As more and more thoughts travel into the void to manifest their understanding of your inspiring Story - pull its vibration into reality - who do you think will be waiting with outstretched strings? Everything is in place for Senida's escape from the Circle, she's already a smoldering, existential probability....' His voice calmed. 'And the wicked after-burn of her exit will instantly destroy The Seed Singer's mind...Need I go on?'

Dreamweaver shook his head. 'It's all just...'

'I know, I know,' interrupted Lynium almost sympathetically. Then he glanced around nervously. 'Look, let me just say this, then we really must get the hell out of here.'

He wiped a few beads of sweat off his brow with the back of his hand. 'Senida has already opened this thing right out, look around,' he made a sweeping gesture. 'You're sitting in her handiwork. The twist that we're stuck with is this: firstly, in order to stop this whole nasty mess from bursting back into reality, we've got to eliminate Senida.' He attempted a wry smile. 'Not so easy I hear you say. But – and this is the icing – we must also rescue The Seed Singer from the dark depths of The Seed.'

Dreamweaver gave Lynium a despondent look. 'Now tell me, where and how do we do that?' he asked in a steady voice. Inwardly he began to feel very afraid. The torment that he had experienced in his Dream-Journeys now seemed almost appealing alongside this Story.

'Ah,' replied Lynium. 'A little tricky.' He paused. 'What the hell... As Senida grew more powerful within the void of possibilities and began unravelling the entire Story from The Seed Singer's force, she finally arrived back at the exact point where he had dragged everything over into the void. And there he sat oscillating deep in trance. As you can imagine, her fury was colossal, but she dare not destroy him before mastering all the techniques necessary for her escape. So she created a fresh crop of the most fearsome Sirens who took his beautiful, damaged body into The Seed; entombing it in a fortress made of pure, conscious evil.'

Dreamweaver's eyes darkened, barely concealing his fear. 'Look, Lynium, I know how much The Seed Singer means to you, and from what I've seen, he is a being of immense value, but even if we achieve the impossible and get to Senida...'

'Dreamweaver,' interrupted Lynium. 'It's not what you think. The Seed Singer expects nothing for himself. However, the situation we are faced with here is far greater than the life of one, even The Seed Singer. No. It is far more serious than that. What we are dealing with is the billions of souls whose imprints are stored inside The Seed Singer's miraculous mind. If The Seed Singer is lost, all of them will be destroyed, and this will have the most catastrophic effect on the entire Universe. Whilst they are safe inside The Seed Singer the Space-Time Continuum can still register their presence, but if they implode into the void, their absence will cause the most enormous vibration-ripple.'

He paused, looking the most serious he'd ever looked. 'If that takes place, the Universe will be so destabilised that not even the hands of Nature and God will make the slightest difference.'

Dreamweaver turned pale, and he could feel his palms becoming increasingly wet. 'It just gets better and better,' he said nervously. 'First I'm saving myself, then I'm saving the world...and now it's the Universe.'

Lynium looked down. 'And that brings me to why I was trying to kill you, Dreamweaver. You see, The Seed Singer came to me the day prior to this cataclysm. He told me in exacting detail what was going to happen, and I sat and wept with his head cradled in my arms. He outlined something else though. He said that his powers would not hold out against Senida forever, and he explained how the pin-point on Earth would expand into the Circle it is now. All this has come to pass. He also told me that a Storyteller would be drawn to the Circle by Senida's power: this too has come to pass. Then he said that the Storyteller would find the key to unlock his mind.'

Lynium gathered his thoughts. 'I asked him what this meant,' he continued. 'And he simply smiled and said, *A key is a strange thing, it can subjugate and liberate. It is only the intention of its keeper that determines the role it will play. The one who finds this key can use it for both.*'

Dreamweaver looked puzzled. 'I can't say this whole thing sounds good,' he mused. 'Not for one moment. But I'm still not clear as to why you wanted me out, I seem to fit the description in every respect.'

Lynium smiled. 'All but the most crucial one,' he said. 'The Seed Singer said that the one who unlocks his mind will be...' He hesitated, then said firmly: 'A woman.'

'A woman?'

'Those were his words, and I still don't know what the hell I'm doing here with you,' said Lynium. 'Like I said, it was just the way you told my story in the magical tongue.'

'Why that?'

'Because The Seed Singer warned me that something like that would happen...again despite the one contradiction it all seems to fit.'

'One last thing,' said Dreamweaver.

'What?'

'All the people I've encountered. Are they real, or are they just figments?'

Lynium thought for a second. 'Well it's like this,' he replied. 'Most of what you see is a figment, however, amongst these there are projections of real souls who exist in The Seed Singer's mind. They don't realise they are projections and react as though they are fully immersed in reality. I'm fortunate,' he added. 'Although I'm technically dead, I too exist in The Seed Singer, but he was able to give me some additional powers of projected awareness.'

Dreamweaver nodded. 'I see.'

Lynium smiled. 'You want to know about the kid?'

'No,' replied Dreamweaver. 'I know what I think, and that's all that counts for now.'

'I know what you mean,' said Lynium.

'So what's our first move?' asked Dreamweaver.

Lynium studied the air. 'The first thing is to somehow obtain a couple of Spirit-Codes. For this we'll need to travel to a Seed-Portal based on Earth. That is, Earth five hundred years before you came on the scene. Then we head for the Fortress of Hate.' A thin smile broke across his lips. 'If we get that far we won't have to worry about finding Senida.' Then he laughed. 'And remember, leave the directions to me, and please watch where you're going this time. We don't want to draw too much attention to ourselves right at the start. Now, we must move.'

Dreamweaver lifted his head out of his hands. 'Wow, this sure is one hell of a mess I've got myself into. One hell of a mess.'

17

In the crystalline realm of The Seed, time dared not stir its erosive loins. No darkness; no hint of entropic arrogance; no sub-atomic stir in the light; no creature pertaining to life moved in the somnambulistic radiance >>>> and time not passing >>>> never passing....

Inside a sheath of light-conscious visuals, Senida lay stretched on her back like a carven figure on a tomb... melting through (space).

The dream-ridden spectre of one of her most treasured Warriors bled through the mezmerous seal that separated time from timeless. He stood motionless gazing at the Goddess through acid yellow thoughts, his powerful sound-bitten face glowing with a diamond clear lust.

Pushing through the sheath, he laid his hands on her visual. He spoke, yet his words moved in no form that time could comprehend >>>>>

'Dreamweaver grows more troublesome, my Goddess, and we have also tracked Lynium in the system. It would seem that they are together. I would like to deploy our forces into the fiction wilderness.'

Senida listened, her eyes streaming with alien magic, fixed on the Warrior's flickering spectre.

'Oh, is that really necessary,' she said flatly. 'This whole thing is becoming so tiresome, if a Goddess can become tired.' Her eyes flashed angrily. 'We have nothing to fear from Dreamweaver, he possesses no power. Despite a malfunction in Talis and the business with Lynium, the Storyteller has proved himself clumsy and foolish. His reputation is undeserved… A laser-sharp mind… Per!' she scoffed. 'I really don't know how he managed to enchant so many.'

She floated upwards. 'Unfortunately, it does pose the problem of luring another Storyteller into the Circle.'

The Warrior hovered uneasily. 'With respect, Great Goddess, it is my opinion that we must destroy them at all cost…'

'At all cost!' screeched Senida. 'A little dramatic, don't you think? Who generates all this fake reality for you to act out your evil fantasies?' She glared at the Warrior. 'Me!' She snapped caustically. 'ME!' Then she spun to face him in a shimmering cloud. 'And besides, he's really quite handsome for a mortal… and seeing as we have him here.' Her face clouded. 'No, no, no.' she said. 'I must remember what happened after the last unfortunate coupling with one of those, I'm still paying for it.'

'Shall I deploy our new Cyborg-Witches, Great Goddess?'

'Yes,' Senida laughed with evil relish. 'Oh, yes, now that is going to be fun to watch on the psychic network.' She scowled at the Warrior. 'I don't want any mistakes mind you. I want you to bring them to me for torture and destruction.' Her eyes flashed. 'I shall particularly enjoy saying goodbye to Mr. Lynium… again.'

The Warrior's eyes drank in the image of Senida. 'I shall flood the entire Seed with the hatred of the Great Goddess.'

Senida shook her head. Dream-ghosts flickered and flew into eternity.

'So soon, and already your first error,' she said calmly.

The Warrior flushed transparent. 'Great Goddess?'

'Have you become so human that you will empty the entire sea to catch one fish?' she asked with annoyance. 'All our power must be focused on the target. The Seed is equipped with the intelligence we need to realise our purpose, so we must utilise its resources. Only when the great resurrection has come will we lavish a total destruction. Then, and only then, will our Technology form the core. Then all creatures devoid of Spirit-Code will instantly vanish like unmarked thoughts.

Without a thread to lead them to some earlier misery, without the memory of life there is no fragment to grow into a world. As light is the emissary that carries thoughts between stars, we are the bringers of Immortality; that is the only truth.'

She stared into the Warrior's eyes. 'Don't you agree?'

'Yes... Great Goddess.'

She continued. 'The pathetic nature of mortality sickens me to the core.'

She waved her hand and a soft, milky cloud appeared. She peered in and gazed at the streets of a small town. Then zoomed in further to a family sitting together around a fire crystal.

'Look at them.'

The Warrior peered into the cloud nervously. 'Great Goddess, most of these creatures are possibility-projections.'

Senida smiled. 'Don't be so sure, more of The Seed Singer is pouring out. Besides, I have made it so that their fiction-souls suffer even more – they think finite, they *are* finite. They suffer so much. And when the great resurrection is finished...' She howled with laughter, and The Seed crawled with thick shadows of hate.

'Yes, Great Goddess.'

Not content, she continued. 'Look at what it is to be finite. They cannot dare admit that they are empty space formed into flesh by nothing more than sound. Their terrestrial base has become so weak that they oscillate uncertain of what to think themselves into. I allow only a chosen few into my paradise, yet it seems that even they cannot leave their earthly tragedy. Their weakness disgusts me.'

She became preoccupied, then remarked: 'The Seed Singer could work with this defect and turn weakness into power.' Her voice was huge and metallic, like blunt-edged cutters.

'Then we may yet need to fear him,' cautioned the Warrior, as Senida's light became the blood of his subtle body.

She measured her words carefully. 'The Seed Singer should not be ignored, nor underestimated, as those vile creatures may yet move to worship him more than us >>>> and when humans abase themselves before him, their energy breeds; places filled with love and respect flourish in time and void alike. Order will ferment and the erosion of our power will begin >>>> we see that The Seed Singer is a hideous evil, an abomination that we must destroy.... Yes, we see.'

The Warrior's eyes flashed. 'Then we must destroy him and watch the collapse of Earth and the Universe from the safety of eternity.'

Senida remained expressionless. 'To the poverty of flesh The Seed Singer is both the orchard and the golden apple >>>> the myth and the sayer all in one. The people call after him as if he is the raging Venus that carries all promise in their destruction. It's as though a light that cannot be extinguished burns in their soiled, uncomfortable flesh.'

The Warrior looked concerned. 'Sometimes,' he said. 'To witness how our powers of instantaneous liberation no longer charms them fills my Spirit-Code with a strange wonder >>>>>>>>> Then...NOW I am perplexed. Can we bear to conceive that we will be like this forever, the same substance, no births; no new life; only the things we fake....?

no children........ no need of children...

no children.......   No children......'

The warrior grew dark and silent. There was a flicker of sadness on Senida's face, a kind of falter in her ghost-beauty form. Thoughts darted across her eyes like sparkling fish in a pool of light.

'You are somehow polluted,' she whispered.

The Warrior stammered. 'Ye... Yes, the impossible has happened and I.... feel affinity for The Seed Singer.... Great Goddess.'

Senida looked at him disbelievingly. 'Oh no,' she said seriously. 'I told you to be careful, damn you... you stupid fool. You have become vulnerable...'

He laughed. 'You know something,' he said. 'You know, I think you're really scared, Senida. Part of you is really scared.'

....and there was a kind of lightness in him now, a pure pleasure in his impossible form....

Senida stared in disbelief. 'Blast you, Seed Singer,' she hissed. 'Blast you to my hell. He was my best Warrior...'

'I can see what you saw, Great Goddess, feel your thoughts as you headed towards Earth,' chuckled the Warrior.

From a distance the Earth glows peaceful and serene, but as I draw close, I see something else begin to manifest. This world will fit me, it is hideous, mad and cruel. Every creature shrieks as another consumes it. The wondrous mother landscape floats upon fire...fire that can spew to the surface and incinerate the very life it creates. Yes, the Earth will fit my purpose. Men and women, lost in their own self obsessed misery, savage their host and copulate. They burn and eat the very beasts that their children adore. So perfect: they cannot see a way out of it.

The Earth is so beautiful.

The warrior reached out to touch Senida. 'But you only saw what you wanted to see, didn't you? The Seed Singer has something that can wipe your vision clean and.....'

Senida felt the Warrior's touch as her thoughts annihilated him.

'Enough...enough,' she said in a tired voice. 'It is enough.'

18

The sun had just risen. Dreamweaver was staring into the Circle, and Lynium was making some last minute adjustments to his prosthetics. They were delayed because Lynium wasn't happy with the pattern sequences in the Circle. It was crucial that they were perfect. Just one slight imperfection would send them crashing into oblivion, lost in endless abstractions. Staying put was a dangerous game though, so neither were surprised when the moving mass came over the level plane. The Warriors at the front and flanks, with a multitude of Cyborg-Witches flying above the horde.

The distance seemed to dance and ripple in the rising heat; there was no sound except the gentle swish of portable Spirit-Technology generators. But they announced more with their visuals, the mass flaring so brightly that they could see nothing beyond it. In seconds the vanguard was flowing like oil across the middle ground. A powdery sun imploded into a bubbling hemisphere. The sky turned to night and stars shone like angry pulses casting an eerie glow across the landscape.

Soon the immense plain seemed filled by an ominous swarm... the ground shook as if a million stampeding beasts were moving forward.

And so the day began...

Lynium's face grew drawn, as if the sight had drank his blood. Dreamweaver was close enough to feel Lynium trembling. 'Is this the first time you've met them in solid form?' he asked.

'You know what they say,' replied Lynium. 'Those who risk nothing are rewarded with comfort.'

Dreamweaver Laughed. 'Well it looks like this curse hasn't got far to fly. What about the Circle?'

Lynium stared into the arabesque features as they spiralled into a gaping nothing. 'I won't bore you with the good news,' he said.

Dreamweaver edged over and stared into the swirling pattern. Suddenly his mind was gripped by a hail of stimulus…

A face became a sparkling odour ~ a young girl's eyes became a spaceship hovering like a lost spirit ~ an invented animal became a prayer on a lover's lips ~ endless beauty became impaled on a stem of never being ~ two opposites became utterly mingled ~ a flower screamed inside a dream ~ the flesh of a forbidden journey ~ a cause was suddenly the cure of its own cause.

Lynium pulled him away. 'Hey! Take it easy, Dreamweaver,' he shouted. 'Let's not lose you before the action has even started. I've never seen the pattern so disturbed, it can only be the Sirens blocking our escape.'

Dreamweaver shook his head. 'Hell, what's going on in there?'

'I think it might have something to do with our guests,' Lynium replied, gesturing towards the pursuing juggernaut of hate that was almost upon them.

'Now what do we do, Lynium?' demanded Dreamweaver. 'I don't know about you, but the last time I took on a thousand mechanised demons…'

Suddenly, a great slab of hypnotic sound bellowed out from behind them. They turned to see the Circle's patterns churning with a vivid mass of silver flames. The sound felt like life cast backwards as it washed over them. Streams of brilliance radiated from deep within the Circle. A heavy pillar of light rose from the conflagration and a body-shape emerged from this alchemised quicksand. The light fell away in great splintered shards to reveal the figure…

'Talis,' whispered Dreamweaver. 'Talis.'

She walked out of the flames like crumbling acid. But this wasn't the same Talis that had drifted out of Dreamweaver's hazy vision. He stared into a being cloaked in gleaming kinetic dreadlocks. They danced across her strong face which was white like salt. She carried a look of such fierceness and pride it took his breath away. Her arms and torso, rippling with fine, tectonic slabs of muscle sent seismic shocks through her flesh with every movement. Her Spirit-Code persona grew around her in a radiant simile: it was Goddess and machine made one. A seamless loop of imagination summoned together without corruption of image or rhythm. She was death and resurrection made one.

Her powerful limbs were sparingly clad in magnificent materials of crimson and silvery-blue with a deep vivid purple. There were patterns, and pictures of snarling nethermost beasts made from precious stones of astonishing size and brightness.

A vast, gleaming lust poured from her eyes...

Lynium fell backward with shock and immediately morphed both arms into a clumpy arsenal of exotic weapons.

Talis cast a watchful eye in his direction. 'Save it, Lynium,' she said calmly. 'You're pointing them in the wrong direction.' And with that she lifted her arm and spun Lynium around as though he was a child. 'There,' she said. 'That's better.'

He didn't bother to remonstrate, deciding to accept his fate.

Dreamweaver looked at her breathlessly. 'Talis,' he said. 'What the hell's happened...?'

'It looks like you could both do with some assistance,' she said. 'And luckily I was just passing through.'

She motioned towards the Circle. 'Now you can both go. I've stabilised the pattern,' she said in a hard and sensual voice. 'Go! What are you waiting for? Go!'

Several Cyborg-Witches, ahead of the rest, flew towards them. 'You are finished,' they screamed.

Talis looked up casually and said: 'Actually, it's you that's finished.'

Next, the Witches were a floating cremation, and Talis hadn't even lifted a finger. Without a word she stepped forward and clasped Dreamweaver's arm. She raised her other hand and held his jaw. He felt her kiss, warm and sweet on his face, rich with the perfume of unknown chemicals. Dreamweaver moved to her pushing his mouth onto hers and they locked in a passionate embrace. Then she let him go and her eyes blazed with seductive dreams. She was like a creature with endless lovers, shrewd and adventurous.

They parted and her lips stayed open as if she wanted to do it again.

'Is this who you are, Talis?' asked Dreamweaver.

She smiled tenderly, almost like a young girl bashful at being asked a telling question. 'Let's just say I'm full of possibilities,' she said.

He stepped back. 'Maybe we need to reconsider some of your advice,' he said.

Talis sent up an arc of spiritual flames dispatching five more Witches. She looked puzzled. 'Tell me, Dreamweaver?'

He smiled. 'The more you feel like you belong, the more you will belong,' he said.

Solid silver tears rolled across her cheeks. 'Now look what you've done, Storyteller,' she said 'Do you know how long it took me to put these flames around my eyes.' She gathered her emotions. 'Earth is waiting for you both, the pattern is now perfect. I'll hold this nightmare off as long as I can.'

She was like a blazing light in the distance, coming nearer and nearer. She spoke again. 'Now we really begin,' she said.

Another flock of Cyborg-Witches swooped down on them from above, and Talis torched them with a single glance.

'Now we really begin,' repeated Dreamweaver. 'I...'

'We must go now, Storyteller,' said Lynium, gently taking hold of Dreamweaver's arm. Then just as they leapt into the unknown, Lynium turned to Talis.

'It's good to be wrong,' he shouted.

She smiled as she obliterated another Witch. 'Don't make it a habit now, will you?'

And with that the two men leapt into the Circle and dissolved into the patterns.

'Gone,' she whispered.

She turned her attention to the volley of nightmares spread out in front.

She watched as the mass surrounded the Circle. Vile weapons made of pure evil were growing inside the cloudy womb of a Dream Maker. And from this same ethereal soup, diverse and magnificent fighters crystallised into form and walked into the wilderness. Their limbs flowed like streams of glistening darkness; neither alive nor dead, unfettered by the predicament of existence, making them the most terrifying force ever conceived.

The regiments splayed out in a large circle with the most fearsome Warrior facing Talis. He was fully equipped for the most extreme conflict. There was no time to linger, he had work to do.

Without warning he lifted into the air and flew a full circuit of the area. Then gliding back to the ground he laughed sending a huge disturbance rippling through the air.

His succulent, feminine eyes were peeled with laser destruction; no words could describe the chaos they contained. He was a rampant creator, an awesome, fighting symbiant. Nothing was certain. This avatar of plasma and piercing hate froze all movement in the wilderness.

This was a stand up fight for eternity. And they all knew it.

Talis blinked, and the vast, malignant Spirit-Demon spoke first in a thudding, hypnotic voice. 'This isn't looking good for you, Talis,' he bellowed. 'First you violate your purpose and aid the Storyteller with classified information.' He smiled a powerful, wicked smile. 'And now this.'

Talis shrugged. 'Hmm, you know, I never was one for towing the line… really.'

'Looks like we've got ourselves a situation then,' said the Warrior. 'You see, it's like this: some are destined to be masters and some to serve. If you look closely you will see the beauty, the pure simple beauty of your destruction. Even with Spirit-Technology, the rule of the jungle endures; the strongest will always triumph…'

'Yeah… sure,' Talis yawned. 'Can we just do this?'

The Warrior's eyes flashed angrily. Scores of Cyborg-Witches twitched at his side.

The wilderness remained still, neither side moved.

'Ahhhhhhhhhh'

With a blinding flash… Five of the most powerful Cyborg-Witches flew at Talis blazing with evil thoughts. Talis soared into the sky her eyes launching a beam of coruscating light.

Five brilliant corpses fell at the Warrior's feet.

Without pause, a second gleam of darkness followed, this time rupturing Talis' light-shield in two places. The burning mantras crashed through her Spirit-Code in a wave of sorrowful moans, and their darkness raged into a nightmare of devastation.

Talis absorbed the hit, immediately reworking her symmetries. She knew the crisis was upon her, and with a deafening cry she started to fire into the army from all sides, floating forward, a Ghost-Weapon in each hand.

Her response ignited the battle. Suddenly everything was firing, sweeping vast shadows of suffering across the land in a hunger of destruction. In an instant, the entire wilderness was filled with war. Synthetic Spirits howled, Demons spat fire, Dark Neroids chanted destruction mantras as they floated above the battle, Warriors hurtled through the sky like hell-sent missiles.

Screams – blinding light – every creature on foot or wing exploding with acid fire…

The Warrior gazed through a cloud of preternatural sound as more of his army was destroyed by the sheer determination of Talis' onslaught. Their collapse didn't stop the weapons though; they roared on. But now, several Cyborg-Witches fell to their knees, heads bowed in reverence to Talis.

'Don't kill us, Talis,' they pleaded.

Talis' ears were deaf to their pleading as she rampaged through the sky, twisting like a spinning apocalypse… diamond-cutting shards splaying in every direction.

The Warrior saw this cowardly act and took it upon himself to personally blast the traitorous Witches back into nothing; he would punish their mutiny for the rest of eternity.

'You'rrrrre going dooowwwwwwwwn!!!' he roared, surging into the sky like a missile.

The remaining Cyborg-Witches went into panic mode, abandoning their weapons and hurling their torched darkness at Talis in suicidal terror. She didn't even jerk from the impact. She just carried straight on blasting, eyes fixed in a trance filled with purpose.

She advanced, as more Cyborg-Witches fell to the ground, begging for mercy. She was almost on the Warrior now, who was firing at her with everything he had.

Suddenly, the *invincible* spell was broken, as Talis caught a blast of evil from the Warrior, sending parts of her body into orbit. The back of her head exploded out in a great rope of screams, her iced diamond eyes were shredded to splinters, and her chest gaped open spilling beams of phosphorescent light into the sky.

The Warrior gave a great, shuddering laugh. 'Nothing can defy the Great Goddess and survive,' he bellowed. 'It comes upon you traitor!!!'

Spitting light and dream-blood, Talis looked out through black, imploding eyes. 'It's never... oo...ver til... it's over,' she said in a faltering voice. Then as quick as thought, using shreds of earthly resonance, she performed with sound as a surgeon fashions with tissue and bone, remaking her image from a dancing corona of special effects. Her breathless cipher moved off the ground, different but still deadly...

Crimson shadows cast by the turrets of leaking Spirit-Technology fled across the land like frightened gazelles. The uniqueness of her form drew gasps of admiration. The fighters who'd gathered at either side of the Warrior dissolved into the distance with a single glance, hissing like snakes. But the Warrior turned and dispatched them into nothing with a single hail of fire, and they fell away rotting back into eternity.

Talis stood facing Senida's Warrior; a creature that flowed from a core of menace.

The Warrior scowled. 'You are the interface,' he said. 'You cannot go against your creator, you're a malfunction, Talis, a virus that must be terminated.'

Talis gave a wry smile through her injured persona. 'You Warriors are always so serious,' she offered. 'You should learn to relax.'

In a flash, she let out a blood-curdling scream.....and with a grinding, supernova movement she blasted her assailant into the distance, surging past him, eyes ablaze, locked on her target.

'Now you can relax forever,' said Talis.

The Warrior glanced up staring out from the disaster that was once his face. A twisted smile bled through the churning trash. 'Yo... u're st... st... ill going down,' he spluttered, raising his shadow-gun.

'Gone,' whispered Talis.

The anti-resonance shrunk him to zero...

Talis turned and walked towards the Circle. The earth moaned and churned as her feet touched the ground. The few straggling Witches still remaining active parted silently to let her through, some of them changing into more beautiful incarnations as she passed.

19

Dreamweaver and Peter Lynium moved through a cold street. The shock of first arriving on the Earth which had lain hidden from history was still reverberating in Dreamweaver's head. Somehow, he could more readily accept the miracle-soaking he had encountered on other parts of his strange journey. Even the pseudo-Earth effect of Ge~nes' home had not disturbed him unduly. This was different.

The ooze of teluric, the very aura of this place tugged at his atoms. It was as if every object somehow knew that he was a proper living Earthman, and wanted to touch him, talk to him. He tried to rationalise this, telling himself that it was just another projection, a fake like all the other places vibrating in the Circle. But it bothered him. Lynium had sensed his discomfort and told him to just let it ease off slowly. He had explained that the strangeness would fade into normality, adding in Lynium style: if there is such a thing.

That said, the influence of Senida and her Sirens was everywhere. It seemed that not an aspect of society had been left untouched by their alien hands. For one thing the streets pulsed with Spirit-Technology information systems, which sent Synthetic Souls between Earth and The Seed in tiny conscious Dream-Sheaths. The effect of this bathed the streets in a soft, whispering fog that at first encounter seemed to peer into minds. A spasm of panic gripped Dreamweaver's belly when he had first felt this intrusion. He had dealt with it by breathing deeply and casting his mind back to days spent in the sun with children and animals sitting listening to his stories.

On first arriving, Lynium had quickly stolen some clothes for

Dreamweaver from two men loading boxes onto a floating platform. Lynium had rendered them unconscious by firing a low frequency sound from one of his prosthetic hands. Dreamweaver had thought they were dead, the fog seemed to move towards them, swirling around their heads as though sniffing for a real God-made soul. But in the next instant he had noticed their chests moving and caught the edge of Lynium's knowing glance.

As they had walked through the streets, Dreamweaver's eyes fixed on the architecture. Most of the buildings seemed constructed out of a light-blue plasmeld material which displayed no visible interstice at any point. It was as though the entire structure had been cast from a giant mold. And in keeping with this fashion, great ornamental towers stretched up into the heavens and drifted out of sight through thick, umber clouds.

The streets were crowded with scores of people all going about their everyday business. And for the most part, they looked similar to Dreamweaver's time, an exception being, that some had a slight ashy glow emanating from their flesh. Lynium had explained that these people were taking Spirit-Technology supplements before submitting their bodies to the full Spirit-Code treatment. This guaranteed a far less emotional transition to Immortality, and in some instances, even facilitated the growth of a Spirit-Foetus within the synaptic system.

As they had continued, Dreamweaver occasionally noticed exceptionally perfect-looking men and women floating along on small, gaseous platforms. Moving past, he saw tiny spheres of agitous light hovering in front of their eyes. Lynium had laughed, explaining how this was the mark of status, they were in preparation for high grade Spirit-Codes. He then informed Dreamweaver that the only way to get one of those was to literally "sell your Soul to Senida".

Presently they turned a corner onto a busy main street and walked towards a large plasmeld pyramid, which dominated the panorama.

Dreamweaver looked at Lynium. 'Is that where we're going?' he asked, still feeling a little shaky.

'Now, how did you guess,' answered Lynium sarcastically.

'Glad to see that Earth still brings out that endearing charm,' said Dreamweaver. 'So here's my next stupid question. What happens in there?'

Lynium smiled. 'We sell our Souls to Senida.'

'I knew I shouldn't have asked.'

They moved steadily, Dreamweaver still marvelling at the sight of Earth looking so astonishing. Then suddenly Lynium turned into a small side street, and for a heart-stopping moment Dreamweaver lost sight of him. Then an arm came out of the crowd.

'This way,' said Lynium impatiently.

'I thought we were heading for the pyramid,' said Dreamweaver, looking confused.

'Don't assume anything in this God-forsaken place,' said Lynium. 'We need to make some modifications to our bodies first, and go over a few facts before we continue.'

They moved quickly without exchanging a word, down the narrow street, then followed a high, jet-black wall until they found a door fashioned by scales of violet light.

'One of my old hang-outs,' said Lynium.

He removed the index finger from his left hand and inserted it into a small soft-looking hole punched into the light.

'Walk through it,' ordered Lynium.

Dreamweaver stepped into a small courtyard. A fountain made from a thick blue vapour spurted a crystal clear substance that appeared both solid and liquid at the same time.

'Ah...,' whispered Lynium, 'the miricle of Spirit-Technology...so long since...'

The courtyard was deserted and quiet; an oasis in the wilderness of confusion. They wandered towards a squat, rectangular building and as they approached, the shape of an elaborate façade moved from the structure.

Lynium led them round to a side entrance where a small, shabby door was heavily barricaded. With one mighty blow from Lynium's arm the door surrendered, sending shards of glass and metal into the air.

'What happened to the high-tech lock?' asked Dreamweaver.

Lynium frowned. 'That's the problem with technology... when it lets you down, it really lets you down.'

He pushed the splintered remains apart and gently fed himself in through the gap. Then peering out he said. 'Well, don't wait for an invitation, come in.'

Dreamweaver squeezed through, and watched as Lynium sealed the tear with scraps of metal and wood.

The interior was a schizophrenic mix: mirrors, extraordinary organic shapes carved from crystal alongside decrepit furniture hanging with rot and neglect. It was as if these objects had shared some manifest mastery over time, and now the chinks of light had dragged them away from their autistic slumber. The place reeked of a former life, shadowy odours of activity hanging in the air.

Lynium walked over to a wall at the far end of the room. Curls of yellowed paint were parting company from the plaster and several large, untidy gashes scarred its surface. This time Lynium removed his entire left hand. Dreamweaver watched as he placed the hand on the wall. Then he watched in amazement as it crawled towards one of the gashes like some grotesque spider and nudged at a large paint flake before crawling inside.

Within seconds the wall was a swirling mist, which gently dispersed to reveal a room encased behind its trickery. The room flooded with soft light and Dreamweaver saw that almost every available inch of a pure-white wall was coated with meticulous diagrams of Siren anatomy. They were infested with thousands of tiny flashing pins each marking a specific area of functionality on the Sirens' spectacular form. Each diagram was surrounded by a profusion of high-resolution images of different Warriors and events: strips of sequential images depicting a Siren giving birth to a Warrior, minute thumbnail images of eyes and strange devices.

To Dreamweaver, these were both disturbing and mesmerising in the same instant, displaying a clearly visible pattern that resembled a map of sorts. It was here in this room that Lynium had whiled away the hours trying to uncover the secrets of Spirit-Technology.

Lynium cautiously moved inside as if he was walking into a haunted house. He held up his arm and the hand floated back to its housing.

Dreamweaver moved over to join him.

'Wow, Lynium,' he said breathlessly. 'You're full of surprises.'

Lynium turned. 'Lets hope they're the right kind of surprises,' he said.

He walked over to a small black box attached to one of the few empty spots on the wall.

'Neris,' he said to the box and immediately it grew and morphed into a standing jet-black humanoid figure. It carried all the countenance of a young woman, even down to moist-looking jet eyes encased in jet sockets with jet lids.

Dreamweaver jerked back in shock.

'Status,' said Lynium hurriedly.

'Uncompromised, Peter,' replied the figure in a friendly, feminine voice.

Lynium looked relieved. 'Neris,' he said. 'I'd like you to meet the Storyteller called Dreamweaver.'

Neris turned and looked at Dreamweaver. 'Very pleased to meet you, Dreamweaver,' she said. 'I hope my activation didn't startle you?'

Dreamweaver looked at her uneasily, and then he chanced a quick smile at Lynium.

'Well,' said Lynium sheepishly. 'Just a small indulgence.'

'Good to meet you too, Neris,' said Dreamweaver.

Lynium turned. 'OK, Storyteller, Neris is going to help us prepare for our journey into The Seed. Now this is very important and I need you to listen very carefully before we start.' He moved over to where two scoop-back chairs rested against the wall and sat down.'

'Please join me, Dreamweaver.' He gestured to the other chair. 'Neris, would you bring us some food and prepare a bath for Dreamweaver.'

Neris smiled sweetly. 'What would you like to eat, Dreamweaver?'

'Ah, you know what I'd really…' He stopped in mid-sentence. 'I'll just have some fruit,' he said.

Lynium focused his attention. 'First we must adapt our physiology to the necessary level of Pre-Spirit saturation. This is a reasonably straightforward procedure involving the consumption of Spirit-based synthetics. However, I do have a slight problem...' He hesitated. 'I was stripped of all Spirit-Code access, and to prevent me reinitialising, my Soul's resonance pattern was corrupted.'

He looked sad and thoughtful. 'Now, for the most part, I've been able to override this effect using a series of intense mantra therapies. Dreamweaver, I need to let you know that I will become unstable in The Seed. All I can do is get you in, take you as far as I can, then the rest is up to you. However I do have…'

'Sorry to interrupt, Lynium, but I must just ask you something.'

Lynium nodded 'Go ahead… ask.'

'You speak about Souls,' said Dreamweaver. 'And about the souls that are stored in The Seed Singer.' He gathered his thoughts. 'Well if each of us has a Soul, and in that respect can be considered Immortal, what is the point of Spirit-Code and The Seed?'

'Good question,' replied Lynium. 'It is a very complex matter to grasp, so I'll try to make it as simple as I can without doing it an injustice.'

He drifted deep in thought…

'It's all centred on the notion of an individualised continuum or self. It can be understood that the Universe is compiled within the body of one single conscious entity. This entity desired to know itself intimately, and to achieve this it created the illusion of separation.'

He fiddled with a strange moving disk on his arm. 'Each manifest sub-entity or self possesses a unique resonance pattern, which can essentially be classified as the Soul. This pattern has been endowed with an unimaginably varied and complex array of facets, which in effect are infinite, therefore classified as Immortal. However, the problem arises when this concept is viewed from a localised position, for in reality the very nature of this Immortality relies on constant change. Therefore, the individual or facet is only preserved through the experiences and patterns it feeds back to the whole before it becomes something or someone different.'

Then leaning forward he said: 'You see, Dreamweaver, Spirit-Code effectively arrests the Soul's development by continually repeating the same facet over and over. Therefore never suffering a gross loss of this one ego-self. And it is this loss of self, so celebrated by all Mystics, that humanity has grown to fear the most. As for The Seed Singer and the Souls he preserves, the crucial point is this: if even one single resonance pattern is taken outside of the whole, the system will collapse.'

Dreamweaver looked concerned. 'Spirit-Technology is really toxic,' he said gloomily.

'Unfortunately it is,' agreed Lynium.

As they both sat thinking, Neris came in with a plate of prepared fruits. 'Please help yourself,' she said, offering it to Dreamweaver.

'Thank you, Neris,' said Dreamweaver, taking the plate and placing a grape in his mouth. It tasted identical to the strange, fermented fruit he'd hungrily consumed with Gen~es.

Lynium continued speaking. 'As you may have noticed, I've collated a vast array of information on the composition of Spirit-Technology.

From what I've discovered, there seems to be no clear-cut way without first destroying Senida. Then we pray that this precipitates a full disintegration.'

He got up and walked over to the wall and pointed to a diagram that depicted a cross-section of what looked like Senida's Spiritual Body. He looked over at Dreamweaver. 'From all my work on this subject, I believe that I've possibly discovered a single point on Senida that will begin the process of her destruction. This point is located in the direct holographic centre of her chest.' He zoomed in with his finger. 'Here.'

'So what if your correct,' probed Dreamweaver, 'how do we strike?'

Lynium smiled. 'Oh, no,' he said. 'A flat-on strike is no good, if only it was that simple. You see, because we're dealing with essentially a non-physical entity, the compromise must take place on an etheric level. That is to say from within the nebulous symmetry of Senida's entity.'

'...Fine,' said Dreamweaver cooly. 'So how do we...I do that?'

Lynium pointed at Neris. 'I was about to come to that. Neris has a few tricks up her sleeve. You won't be without support.' A small flicker of a smile crossed his lips. 'Show Dreamweaver, Neris,' he said calmly.

Neris came to stand in between the two men. Suddenly, she seemed to disintegrate into a million shards of gleaming jet. Then an icy wind swept through the room, blowing papers onto the floor as Neris became a tumultuous conjurement spiralling around Dreamweaver's head, almost faster than his mind could register. By the time he'd blinked, Neris was standing exactly where she had first started with a big smile splashed across her ebonised face.

Dreamweaver let out a shocked laugh. 'God! How the...'

'I can do other things too, Dreamweaver,' said Neris. 'Would you like to feel me pass through your mind?'

'I think we must move on, Neris,' said Lynium, with the mischievous grin still fixed across his carved features. 'I'm sure Dreamweaver will have the opportunity...'

He moved back to his chair. 'Basically, Neris is designed to infiltrate Senida at exactly the precise Spirit-Trajectory to inflict the necessary damage to her matrix of evils. Neris already has an advanced Etheric Modulator to enable her to move freely inside The Seed. Your job, Dreamweaver will be to draw Senida out into a position where Neris can move in on her.'

He cast his eyes down. 'I'm sorry I won't be there to see that.'

'That makes two of us,' said Dreamweaver softly. 'I'm not sure I like my role though, I've gone from being the world's most renowned Storyteller to a piece of ghost-meat dangling on a hook.' He smiled. 'So what's our next move, Mr Outlaw?'

Lynium brightened as if a switch had suddenly flicked. 'OK,' he said enthusiastically. 'Neris will prepare us for our Spirit-Code Insemination.' He paused. 'A word of warning, Dreamweaver: because you're...how shall I say...a virgin.' He smiled. 'You will experience some strange sensations to begin with. They will be unlike anything you've experienced before. For example, your notion of what Time is will dramatically alter. At first, each second will seem to crystallise into a multiplex of beautiful, interlocking patterns. This can have a... somewhat stupefying effect. It can in no way be compared to a narcotic-based experience. All I can say is, enjoy it, don't resist, and you'll soon be able to actually see time like an element, in much the same way that we see water or fire.

'Now, when we're inside The Seed you will actually have the ability to move time - even fashion it into a multitude of different ratios. Although you may experience things in a linear sequence, it is quite possible for the end to take place before the beginning.' He looked concerned. 'The irony of it is, that you have no time to practice. You will just have to use your imagination, hope for the best.'

'Sounds familiar,' said Dreamweaver. 'Is there anything else I need to know?'

'Yes,' replied Lynium. 'When I say use your imagination, I mean exactly that. As with all dimensions, we are only limited by the imagination. However, unlike the third dimension, The Seed has no discernible gap between thought and manifestation. Remember my words,

Dreamweaver: there is no gap between thought and manifestation, so you must use every skill you possess as a Storyteller, every skill.'

Dreamweaver puffed out his cheeks and slowly let out a long, stress-relieving breath. Then turning to Neris he said. 'Can you teach me a few tricks, Neris?'

She looked somewhat puzzled, then her face cleared into a smile. 'Only if you show me some of yours, Dreamweaver,' she said in a brisk voice.

Lynium laughed so much that his hands morphed into great turnip-shaped stumps.

20

Senida floated inside her Spirit-Technology languishing in a post-violent trance.

There was much to displease her... Oh yes... Not least the fact that two of her most advanced Spirit-Codes, those she had personally created, had inexplicably malfunctioned.

The Warrior had been most unfortunate with his joy-soaked personal utterances, but Talis had proved a very costly fault indeed, even though the pleasures drawn from her destruction would contain elements of... stimulation...

Small compensation alongside the damage inflicted to Senida's valuable resources, and the depletion of violence within The Seed's ghostly mechanisms.

Floating deep in trance, Senida tracked through the complex eugenics of the Story. Until now, she had paid little attention to the matter of Lynium's mysterious appearance in her system. Although, from the start, she had noted his smuggled apparition when Dreamweaver had first set foot inside the Circle, she had left this breach of her security untouched. She had preferred to work it to her advantage, adding to the Circle's mystery.

Senida had interpreted Lynium's presence in the visions as a crude gesture from a once great mind, damaged, powerless and without a Spirit-Code. But something in those iced images made her linger for an *eternal* second over his sepia fragments as they bled through her mind. It had been careless of her not to finish him off, she now thought, but at the time, she had relished in his clumsy, corporeal discomfort. She would not allow herself the privilege of a second error...

And there was Dreamweaver. She now explored the possibility that he had twisted something in Talis, that he possessed hidden talents bestowed by The Seed Singer. *No... No... Surely not*, she thought. *Surely not...*

Yes, yes... she had it! Lynium had corrupted Talis... yes... what... was he up to... no he couldn't have the resources... yes... no... yes...

But how could Dreamweaver be the clumsy fool she'd tagged him for, blundering from one disaster to another? He'd escaped an army of Warriors and Cyborg-Witches through the help of Talis... wait... wait...No... ((((her mind spun through image after image))))....

Her eyes froze. And where were they now???... Disappeared... Lynium, Lynium... Dreamweaver... What would he do?... They were together... What were they up to???.. What... what?????

No...they wouldn't dare....

She was infinitely powerful, the Great Goddess, why should two renegades pose a threat?

But they did...

In the trance, she cast her thoughts back to the 'corrupted' Warrior and zoomed in on his mind, replaying his words, "I think you're afraid". Maybe here, in the innermost reaches of synthetic consciousness... clues... clues.

She wasn't attaining to Goddesshood; she was the Goddess who reigned supreme.

'Warrior!' she screamed. 'Warrior, now!'

A fractal wave ripped through Senida's trance like a great fist punching the fabric of space, and a Warrior hovered inside her mind.

'Yes, Great Goddess,' he said, sending a billion echoes into Senida's thoughts.

She was now in a state of extreme agitation. The Warrior's sudden appearance enraged her, causing his immediate disposal as a burning, eternal corpse. 'AAAAAAAhhhhhhhhh!' she bansheed. 'Another Warrior!'

A second Warrior slipped cautiously through the ethereal scrim. 'You called, Great Goddess.'

Calming herself, Senida clutched at the Warrior's spiritually muscular form. 'Warrior,' she gasped. 'Listen to me, listen... I want Dreamweaver and Lynium terminated AT ALL COSTS! Do I make myself clear?... AT ALL COSTS!

'Yes, Great Goddess,' replied the Warrior passionately.

He left his form behind, becoming visions in other minds, sending a slice of Synthetic Spirit coursing through The Seed then sweeping down across Earth. The message was clear and precise.

Senida looked out of The Seed down upon the Earth, sparkling and blue, and for a barely registered instance she seemed to falter. She felt this and it terrified her to the core...

'Is this something I need to know?' she asked herself...

Blue... just... blue... 'Dreamweaver,' she whispered. 'Dreamweaver. I know you, Dreamweaver....'

She smiled. 'Yes, it comes to me, it comes to me.'

'Warrior,' she called.

A Warrior stood before her.

'Warrior, I want you to cancel that last command,' she said in a soft, calm voice. 'Cancel the order I gave to eliminate the renegades.'

A look of surprise flashed across the Warrior's face. 'I... I don't understand.'

Senida smiled softly. 'Just do it.' Then she added: 'Please.'

The Warrior's image faltered. 'Yes, Great Goddess.'

21

At the intersection of wall and ceiling ran a ring of dazzling screens, a halo circling a jewelled skull. Bright as they were, they emitted a soft, ghostly haze which drifted down over Neris as she diligently worked at transforming the two men.

Half-concealed by a mire of Spiritual equipment, Dreamweaver's eyes stared out bleached and disbelieving. Without shifting, they followed the paths of complex scrawls of plasma, rich in detail, as they knitted sparkling thoughts together. At first sight, these perceptions had seemed so pure that Dreamweaver's gaze seemed like some demon clasping at angels.

Neris drew close to Dreamweaver. 'You're a song of stars, Neris,' he whispered.

Neris smiled. 'I can see that the Spirit-Supplements are taking effect, Dreamweaver,' she said.

Regrettably, Lynium's prosthetics were reduced to a spumey mess by the addition of the supplements to his system, and Neris gave him a concerned glance.

'It's not looking good, Peter,' she said calmly. 'I suggest we move over to the new chakra-system. The Sirens made a good job of disturbing your soul's resonance.'

Lynium peered down at himself. 'Do whatever it takes to keep me in there for as long as possible,' he said in a strained voice. 'I'll worry about putting things back together when I...if I return.'

Dreamweaver felt his awareness creeping around other planes, exploring new types of thinking, new styles of being. At one stage, Neris injected something into the top of his head, and for some time after he had felt his body melting away like heated wax. He felt grown, expanded through quivering space.

Neris looked at him from a great distance. She was shouting something. She was shouting something, but he was walking towards a piercing light, nothing could stop him, and there in front was the entrance to a different truth. Then he walked out and the movement of his body was vivid and clean like the tension between bone-white knuckles. It felt good, really good.

The diaphanous landscape that came to greet him engraved its presence by placing coloured ghosts in his head. He looked across a busy street, somewhere lost in time's grasp. People moved very slowly along a mist-swathed street. They turned and looked at him, their eyes filled with a nether-world glint, skin soft and phosphorescent. He looked up into a deep, sapphire blue sky quenched by rays from a silent corona. In this vast untamed cityscape he discovered horizons he'd never seen. Millions of beings were following a destiny they would never understand. The banality, the grasping, senseless exchange. Any purpose was beyond his understanding, though it was clear that meaning lay behind each tiny drama. Time didn't pass, never passed – nothing to be, nowhere to go.... nothing.

He turned in a spreading gauze of slow motion and walked into a tall plasmeld building. He passed a woman walking backwards in time – her body made from emptiness. He tried to touch her and his hand passed straight through her body. He pulled out her Soul and it was beautiful and sparkled with magic. A young boy walked past holding his mother's hand, crying solid silver tears. A woman and a man laughed and drank from time. The girl dripped her body into the man's Soul.

Dreamweaver... Dreamweaver.... Dream-Weaver... Dream... he turned his gaze away from the girl's lips, yet he wanted to taste her sweet, innocent time. Her eyes shone with forever and her face pierced his mind, a rampant glow with insane thinking effects.

Everything his eyes met looked astonishing, but he felt the pain of sadness because he knew in his heart they were forever irredeemable.

Images as real as granite surrounded him, but when he touched them they became like sunlight on a lover's face, so beautiful, so fleeting – lost in the stark ambition of Time.

He walked into a large room filled with milky light. People moved around him, through him, instead of him. The room was garnished with a huge, moving fresco where, in hypnotic slow motion, a tribe of women danced in a glowing forest.

Their limbs were powerful, lithe and perfect as if fashioned by magic, and he could smell a rich febrile odour hovering from their skin, moving from the painting. Trails of silver-blue hair fell from their heads, blazing like comet's tails. The women sang as they danced, and their voices were raw and putrid like rotting flesh – yet they mesmerised, conjuring strange yearnings in his mind.

The song swirled in an endless round, on and on, each time gathering strength. It was music to grow lost in, and their fiery, galvanised faces glistened like polished amber.

The dance grew frantic...

Suddenly, one of the women leapt into the centre of the throng. She tore off the strip of cloth that covered her sex, and stood naked in front of him. Her face was wild, feline with delicate spirals gauged in the flesh. She held out her left hand, and in it appeared a book. Its cover glimmered like dark crystal. She held the book out in front of her.

She moved smoothly, the book carving circles in the air. Then she shook with wild, chaotic movements; suddenly she stopped: then she took the book and gently handed it to him in slow motion...

He reached out to take it.

She stared out of the fresco straight into his eyes.

'Open it,' she said softly. 'Open it...'

She was a promise returning to form. She had the appearance of life passing through on its way to something brilliant. It was a face so full of love and purpose that all realms wished it for their own.

'Open it, Dreamweaver,' she implored.

'What is this book?' he asked.

She smiled a beautiful knowing smile. 'It's the Story, Dreamweaver. The Story you came to get. Have you forgotten?'

He looked bemused. 'Yes, I remember there was a Story.'

'You're still confusing what you see with what is really happening,' she said.

'Who are you?' he asked abruptly

She smiled. 'Look into the book, it will show you,' she whispered. Then she smiled. 'No, better still, look at how it ends, I know it's cheating but I want you to know.'

Her eyes sparkled… He opened the book and looked down… he read…

The stupendous action had been shed. Deep in the womb of The Seed, the process I had instigated was just beginning. I wondered if a time would come when the real maker of Eternity would reveal herself; a time when humans and Sirens had learnt to be with the truth – the delicious cycle of demolishing truth that forms all that we must lose in the raptures of endless change.

I heard someone behind me – first a child's laughter, then a question.

'Why are you crying, Dreamweaver?'

Dreamweaver turned and looked at a little girl. Cascades of shiny blue-black hair framed a slim and delicately boned face; she was no more than eight or nine. Her eyes were green, slightly slanted and soulful. She was beautiful.

'I never made it back. I have something that doesn't belong to me.' He held up a tiny golden Soul-Casket.

'May I look inside?" asked the little girl.

Dreamweaver looked up. 'How do you know I'm called Dreamweaver?'

The little girl's eyes flashed and she laughed. 'Oh, we've met before,' she said sweetly. 'I told you to recognise who and what, in the midst of the chaos, was not chaos, then to believe in that, making it vital and beautiful.'

He stared at her and watched in vivid holographic detail as she broke apart and a creature emerged from the hollow flesh-shell. A creature half serpent, half-human: a Serpent-Girl, blue luminous beads for eyes, skin like golden sequins and two spiralled serpent fangs grafted to her upper mouth. Suddenly his entire mind was filled with her luscious feminine tongue. Her evil energy pulsed through time and the girl began to rock back and forth. A hypnotic sound broke from her lips now open to the glistening fangs, her breath blazed like a comet.

She spoke and stars shot from her eyes. 'Let me read it for you, Dreamweaver.' She reached up and pulled words from the air.

A painful constriction gripped The Seed. Shadows fled from their makers to hide in thinking ghosts. They rolled and twisted through streets of melting visions. Senida had defeated everything, annihilated every breathing creature. Dreamweaver threw himself down absolutely aware that there was no point in trying to escape.

It was of course too late..... The mission to liberate the billions of Souls from The Seed Singer's mind had failed.

Ghostly light ~ beyond the super-set ~ death's light-speed eyes drink the paradise of silence

~ I am burning ~ we are consumed ~ falling ~ falling

~ falling

~ falling

~ falling....

Suddenly, Dreamweaver threw out his hand and caught a shard of light nestled in the dark flames. He stabilised himself and began to pull the light into a bigger shape. He pulled and stretched it until he was able to climb through it.

He stood in front of the Serpent-Girl.

She glared at him. 'You die, Dreamweaver!' she screamed. 'You don't make it, you die!!!'

Dreamweaver smiled. 'Not this time,' he said.

'You didn't make it!!!!!!!!!!!!!!!'

He turned and walked away from the evil creature. Then he stopped and looked back.

'Part of you wants me to make it,' he said.

'You're dead, Storyteller....... dead!!!!!!'

With that he walked away. The fresco moved and shimmered as if it was alive. He moved through the room, along a thin dimly lit corridor. He sensed someone by his side.

He turned.

'Let me do the talking, Storyteller,' said Lynium. 'Keep that stupid storytelling mouth shut, OK.'

Dreamweaver laughed. 'You know something, Outlaw, I never thought I'd be happy to hear that miserable voice.'

Lynium smiled. 'Ha,' he snapped. 'That new face looks good on you, have you thought of maybe keeping it?'

Dreamweaver stared back at him. 'I could say the same,' he replied sharply.

Neris had performed a miracle on his face. She had taken at least ten years off Lynium's age, and he now seemed almost mulatto. His hair was now longer and thicker, his teeth gleaming white and his eyes a radiant green. His skin looked smooth and relatively blemish free. Neris had paid fastidious attention to the minutest of details and to complete his metamorphosis there was the slight glow of Spirit-Technology, which oozed from deep within his being. Neris had mind-sculpted atoms rendering her handiwork undetectable by even the most advanced Spirit-Technology scanners.

She had paid no less attention to Dreamweaver, although he had felt less comfortable with her rendition. She had fashioned him with long straight hair the colour of fresh drawn blood, which fell across a fast, deadly and almost feminine face. The features felt wonderful though, and seemed to move like speeding thoughts, clipped and smooth. Lynium had explained how this was a typical High-Active Spirit-Persona look and would work their cover effectively. The plan Lynium and Neris had hatched was simple. Lynium would pose as Dreamweaver's Earth-side Spirit-Guide. Lynium had explained to Dreamweaver how new Spirit-Codes often took their first journey into The Seed with a Guide. For the most part, these Guides were required to keep corporeal form and apply for renewed Spirit-Codes at the same time as their clients. This was largely to do with security following a spate of attempted Spirit-Code thefts.

Lynium had thought of everything, and Neris had carefully forged all of the Security Vapours and prepared the Resonance Discs to carry their Soul Patterns. But she had given Dreamweaver a shock when she had asked for his pattern. He had stared fixedly, and was just becoming concerned when Neris gave an impish smile and said, "Just how The Seed Singer said it would be". She had then clasped his jaw, reached into his mouth with a tiny Spirit-Probe and placed it against a tooth. Instantly, he remembered Talis placing the tiny shrine-fragment against the same tooth. A flicker of doubt had passed through him, *how could this match,* but it was quickly washed away in a river of other thoughts.

Presently, Lynium ran his hand over a curtain of frosted light at the end of the corridor. His hand touched his heart, and he stroked Neris who was now cleverly concealed in a Micro-Spirit vessel embedded in his aura.

The light bled away...

They entered a room. Inside, its walls faded into the distance, smeared red with a strange, chattering paste that lived and moved. The movement created a sound that reminded Dreamweaver of Talis' song in his Dream-Journey. It was as if these walls had been anointed for some ceremony or sacrificial practice.

As he looked up, Dreamweaver saw the ceiling was covered for as far as he could see by a fresco. Delicate wisps flew amongst strong-looking celestial men and women, set against an angry cloud-soaked sky. Their skin was ivory – stretched tightly over delicate bones. Stealth features and compelling cheekbones were framed by casques of jet-black hair painted to make it move.

Two vapour chairs appeared either side of a flat sheet of black light. A third chair appeared at the far end; this chair was larger and more elaborately gasious.

A sensual, feminine voice broke through the air. 'Please make yourselves comfortable, Gentlemen,' it said. 'Help yourself to some liquid darkness, an assistant will be with you shortly.'

Lynium gestured for them to sit.

Two frosted pewters rose from the surface of the black light, charged with a heavy, murky fluid.

Both of them looked at the pewters, neither made any attempt to take one.

Without any discernible trace of movement to announce her entry, a young woman with dancing white pneumatic hair and phosphorous skin lowered herself into her waiting chair. She was draped in thin bracelets of light, which gave her the appearance of a bleached angel.

'Welcome, Gentlemen, my name is Xyon~ter, and I will be your Spirit-Code Facilitator.' She smiled releasing a milky cloud from her mouth. 'Now, may I ask you for your vapours and a copy of both Soul Patterns so our technicians can begin processing your Spirit-Codes.'

Lynium reached into his jacket and withdrew a small gummy ball, which he placed on the table in front of him. The ball began to pulse with light, and within seconds, it was a small cloud of bluey gas. The cloud floated over to where the facilitator was sitting. She studied it intensely for what seemed like hours to Dreamweaver. He could feel his new face become twitchy and caught a fractious glance from Lynium. The woman broke away from the cloud and gazed suspiciously at both of them, her shining eyes narrowed.

She seemed to linger on Dreamweaver for an uncomfortable period of time. Finally, she spoke.

'Are you nervous, Mr. Telomere?' she asked in a cold voice.

Dreamweaver rigamorticed. 'Er, yes,' he said calmly. 'It's my first time, as you can see.'

The ice-maiden stare softened. 'Well, Gentlemen, all of your information appears to be in order,' she said, exhuming her illumine voice. 'You may proceed to the Spirit-Code insemination point. From there you will be taken to The Seed transporter.' Then she added: 'Have a nice Eternity, Mr. Telomere.'

And with that, the room evaporated and they found themselves standing in a membrane of sparkling fog. Dreamweaver reached towards it with a probing finger, instantly withdrawing as it hissed with displeasure.

Then a male voice spoke from the fog. 'Mr. Dakini, please ensure that your client is relaxed and comfortable. Your Spirit-Codes are now operational and you will begin your ascension in approximately one minute.'

'Thank you,' replied Lynium. 'We're both ready.' Then turning to Dreamweaver, he said: 'Safe trip Mr. Telomere'

Dreamweaver turned. 'See you on the other side,' he said. Then added: 'Mr. Dakini.'

22

Dreamweaver felt his mind heaved upwards and lifted away from his body, drawn through a chanting darkness. His mind registered a multitude of conflicting data.

Telescopic noise, imploding thoughts, orgasmic flashes of light-soaked pain. Threads of intelligence piercing his veins and arteries, a penetrating golden force.

As he travelled further, the meaning of *alive* dissolved into Spirit-Code. He was taken apart and recreated with new and dynamic forms.

Suddenly, Neris crystallised before him in a wave of thinking fractals. 'Think of yourself, Dreamweaver,' she said. 'Think of yourself.'

He fixed his mind on her words…

Next, a never-ending spectrum of possibilities quarterised and zoomed The Seed into super-sense focus.

He stared through sightless eyes, yet saw detail with more intimacy than anything before. His thoughts struck like tingling glass. The formula for eternal life bulged through multi-dimentions. He gazed across The Seed as a thousand emerald suns emerged from the eyes of moist-winged Demons and spread light across the landscape.

The sparkling beams danced across the Demons' bodies like tendrils of opalescent dreams and filled the landscape with their avatars. Dreamweaver saw how time drifted like sound around their bodies, and how each incarnation reached up and shaped it like watery clay.

In the suns he saw shapes so miraculous and beautiful that none of the Miracles held in the realm of time and matter could ever match their glory… yet they etched his Soul like psychic acid.

He engrossed himself in the wonder-soaked firmament, and felt as if he had emerged from a deceased slumber where nothing had any power to amaze.

'Dreamweaver.'

The voice again.

'Think of yourself, Dreamweaver.'

'How?' he called.

The simple act of him calling caused The Seed to paint him into its endless reality.

He watched as Lynium and Neris shot into focus against a gaping, creative void.

'Nice of you to join us,' said Lynium, in a voice that stretched out forever.

Dreamweaver looked at him. Lynium reached up and pulled a quivering sheet of consciousness from the air and wrapped it around Dreamweaver. Immediately he saw things more coherently.

He tried to speak again. '… I can't…'

Lynium smiled, then motioned to Neris who blossomed into a black cloud, which pierced Dreamweaver's mind.

'Be calm,' she said compassionately. 'I'm going to stabilise you.'

He felt himself slipping into a never-ending plume of images. Then suddenly they galvanised in front of him like water turning to ice.

'There,' said Neris, standing before him.

Suddenly, he moved without moving. Thought holistically without time.

'Always intriguing,' said Lynium.

He now looked almost the same as the Earthbound image Dreamweaver remembered, except he appeared to have an endless array of shapes oozing out from every part of his body, constantly making him, constantly exploring different methods to construct the same end result. He swept his gaze to fix on Neris and saw the same spectacle unfolding.

Lynium reached into the landscape and pulled away chunks of dimension to display different aspects of the vista.

'We're heading through these to get to where Senida has The Seed Singer,' he shouted.

Dreamweaver looked through the parted fold of Seed reality and could make out a vast churning shape unfolding and collapsing back into a blatant and frightening mass of darkness.

'Let's go,' he said,' 'I may even be of some use now.'

Dreamweaver watched with awe as Neris flew into the air and plucked a cloud of empty thoughts. And without moving, she constructed some type of hovering platform.

'This will be fine, Peter,' she said.

'Good,' said Lynium, taking hold of Dreamweaver in a curtain of similes. 'Get on, Storyteller, it's about no-time we got this show on the road.'

A gleaming Seed interface bled from Neris' eyes as she floated onto the newly constructed Thought-Cloud. She was a wish being granted its fulfilment, incredible to observe as she shimmered with ghosts of rich sound, streaming her jet-black chaos across Dreamweaver's mind.

Dreamweaver was completely immersed, sculpting thoughts with a dazzling extended sense – dangerous – immoral – advanced – a flagrant alteration. He looked at Lynium and understood now why he had been drawn to this Circle and why he'd made it to this crashing climax. The Story was the ultimate source of all his stories; the manifest magic of all words and thoughts.

They were flying through The Seed's dream-soaked sky. Talking stars descended from space and shed their gleams in brilliant prose. The three of them were riding into battle, a rack of pulsing chakras. Dreamweaver felt as if he was unravelling into a new type of myth, a myth so vibrant and complex that no number of Storytellers could ever communicate its profound radiance through language or image alone.

Neris merged with the thought-cloud shaping it into their minds, moving them towards the realm of The Seed Singer. The Story was falling into Dreamweaver's head playing each frame through his mind, filling him with images. The Seedscape twisted and the Thought-Cloud mirrored its convolutions, chasing each corner to find the way to Senida's miracle place. The sequence was moving out of its own future, the images were softening with speed, and The Seed's suns were lost to another hemisphere.

They soared over crystal mountains on a spiralling cloud of thought, floating on bodiless winds, descending towards a paradigm realm. Spirit Technology flickered across their psychic eyes like the frames of a whispered chant.

They swept across the strange landscapes, a sparkling tempest drinking in cities below that were moving to vast rhythms. Night fell instantaneously; everywhere darkness enveloped the swirling sky except where they flew. The light from their presence chased across the ground casting silver shadows on huge, sleeping rocks. Rivers became silent, thin, sinuous – the opaque texture of frosted glass. And as they journeyed forth, the cities became more like a living body, alien streets teaming with incredible beings. Lynium pointed to different scenes as they went, explaining something of how things worked. He explained that The Seed was a realm where paradox crystallized into meta-truths, then back into gleaming contradictions: a domain energized by inverted love. Dreamweaver was still incredulous that such a creation could be the work of Senida.

Giant spirit trees stretched their seraphim branches and Dreamweaver steered his fingers to greet them. Immediately, he felt a toxic wave of pain sweep through his Spirit-Code.

'Everything is toxic,' warned Lynium. 'Nothing is what it seems.'

They flew over a vast crystal mountain, swooping down through what appeared to be an ancient spirit-infested forest. This quickly gave way to a dark, jagged landscape, sliced through the middle by a river, which gushed upwards at some unthinkable command. Dreamweaver could feel the river's swirling torrent devouring the land with a sickening violence.

The thought-cloud flew on, lower now, as the strange skape changed again, crowding with more diverse beings. They continued to fly through sheets of colourful reality... And it was then that Neris sensed they were being followed.

'Damn it,' shouted Lynium. 'Senida knows we're here. She must have tracked my old Soul Pattern.'

Lynium had been concerned that this would draw Senida's Warriors to them. Neris had skilfully masked it with a new pattern, but the act of entering The Seed must have shaken the old pattern free.

'What now?' asked Dreamweaver.

'No matter,' responded Lynium, 'it just means we'll be meeting a little resistance to us reaching Senida's Temple.'

Neris gushed from the thought-cloud. 'Peter, this looks worse than I anticipated. I'm picking up a large number of Warriors and a clutch of Cyborg-Witches heading our way.' She looked at Lynium, concerned. 'The other piece of good news is your Spirit-Code is starting to become unstable. I'm not sure how much longer I can keep you here, Peter.'

Lynium turned to Dreamweaver. 'It's getting close, Storyteller.'

Dreamweaver was calm and collected. He was piecing this myth together now, and nothing was going to stop it taking place. He reached over and touched Lynium's Seed Persona.

'Stay as long as you can, Peter,' he said. 'But I want a decent meal in that place of yours, so don't think of doing anything stupid.'

Lynium smiled. 'And have you complaining that it all tastes the same.'

Neris came back. 'Just to make you both aware, we're about to be joined by Senida's reception committee.'

With this, she pulled a ball of fractals from inside her abdomen and quickly shaped them into three pistols. 'You'd better take these,' she said, 'they're Spirit-Eating Weapons. I get the distinct impression we're going to need them, but don't rely on them. Most of Senida's crew are able to absorb these rays without sustaining too much damage, but they'll buy us some no-time. At this poi…'

The first of their pursuers appeared from the landscape below; Eight Cyborg-Witches bathed in a deep tellurium sheen rapidly closed the distance between them. The Witches feasted on the scent of Lynium's ruptured Soul.

Neris flew them down to where a multitude of other Spirits could possibly act as a shield. They were lucky, this particular shard of The Seed crawled with a multitude of different beings. Dreamweaver saw an endless line of sparkling personae moving towards Senida's Temple. Some were elegant Transforms, fashioned as Sirens or Warriors, others more spiritual-like, hovered on Ghostly Cyborgs, their features made from dense, rhombic patterns. Others flew on alien essences draped in long, flowing thoughts, while more still, were just elaborate sound, bursting with dangerous movements. All of them carried a strange malignancy, a sense of unashamed malice.

The moving droves of Concept-Creatures could act as camouflage. If they flew without time it would cloak them before their pursuers could capture the pathway.

They continued like liquefied shock moving towards Senida's Temple. Scanning the horizon, Neris noticed an opening ahead between two columns of solid black flames and steered the Thought-Cloud skillfully through the gap. She then flew them through a multitude of shifting geometries, sending layer upon layer of dense imagery pouring through Dreamweaver's eyes. But they were quickly running out of options as the army of pursuers began destroying everything obstructing their progress. Countless Spirit Constructs suffered at their hands: destined, with no option of death, to experience their agonizing state of ruin for the rest of eternity.

As they plunged through a slab of frozen time, Lynium started to break apart, his connection to The Seed was gossamer fine. But Neris managed to stabilize him using the psychic transference of Spiritual Mathematics. The fractious components of Lynium's body flickered angrily before knitting back together, and as they fused he cried out in agony.

'I'm sorry, Peter,' said Neris, 'It's the only way to keep you here.'

'Just...do whatever's...necessary, Neris,' winced Lynium.

They journeyed on towards Senida's Temple…When, without warning, they pierced an invisible matrix of Sironic Rhythms searching the skies. The Thought-Cloud ground to a halt, and in a blinding flash, the turbulent aura of a Cyborg-Witch bled through a sheet of thought, and hovered menacingly before them.

Dreamweaver studied the Witch, and he found himself admiring the formidable artistry of her form – an explicit asymmetric - a thick sweep of moving shadow which coerced from a body of thinking sound - a gleaming instrument of destruction.

'It's over.' The Witch's voice was precise and handsome; a Demon in her hand was pointing directly at them, warm with intention.

The three of them stood motionless on the Thought-Cloud. Lynium's fingers closed around his Ghost-Weapon. 'They'll have orders to capture us,' he thought from the corner of his mind. 'Senida will want to finish us personally.'

His conviction was proved by the lack of immediate violence in response to his threat: they were still conscious.

Not yet, Dreamweaver said to himself.

'What's it to be?' challenged Lynium, as Neris stood at his side.

The Cybor-Witch was ecstatic, aiming the Demon at their innermost essence, straight and true. A slither of nervous light crept through a canopy of glycerine bodies above, signalling a thick, almost ritual shift across The Seed. Sirens, Warriors and Witches were closing in.

Dreamweaver heard screams of panic, as scores of radiant personae were retired to make way for the fighters. The dense spread of violence, moved across the land in a lexicon of misery. The Warriors floated through bodies, not caring to see the carnage they'd caused. Cold destruction their purpose.

Then, deliberately and slowly Neris levelled her weapon, a fiery ghost – a gleaming messiah of ending – directly at the Witch's mind. Lynium coaxed his weapon from inside his body and matched Neris' aim. Dreamweaver carefully followed suit.

'How's this going to end?' shouted Neris.

The Witch lingered; her psyche fixed on them. Dreamweaver felt her ghostly mouth pressing at his lips - demanding. He watched her livid zeros licked with lust at his thoughts. Then, without warning she gently lowered her Demon, releasing a seething mass of dreams from its chamber – down..... down.... down....like a future passed by time.

They remained motionless - surprised...confused...images....no time.

And when the Cyborg-Witch fixed her gaze on them, something had changed; a new life filled her soul-piercing eyes. Suddenly, from her body's churning curse, there emerged a beautiful woman with skin of glittering sound and compassionate burnished eyes. Dreamweaver had the fleeting impression that he could still see the Witch's features beneath.

Though it seemed impossible, Senida's fatal instrument had lost her appetite for destruction. The Witch held up a slim sharp-nailed hand, which shone like a sapphire. 'Go on your way........ It is enough,' she said, with lightning struck backwards. 'A great change is sweeping across The Seed and it is time to stop all this hate.'

Lynium stared at the others in total disbelief. Neris gently placed her hand over his weapon and lowered it to his side. He offered no resistance; he just kept staring at the Witch in trance-like disbelief.

Neris addressed The Witch. 'Come with us, you know Senida will destroy you for all Eternity, The Seed is over for you now. You belong with The Seed Singer and us.'

'I belong only to a vision,' said the Witch. 'Soon my image will evaporate.' She looked up. 'I never really wanted to exist forever you know.' She then managed a smile and the dark detritus lifted from her new form. 'I want to disappear like a mist caught by the morning breeze, and finally be released. The Demonic Time is approaching its end, I can feel this change inside the very fabric of my being, there is no juice left for misery and destruction.'

Dreamweaver looked into her eyes. 'Tell us why you've stopped?' he asked.

The Cyborg-Witch shook her beautiful head. 'Dreamweaver, you've arrived to find The Seed changing, as the tide turns, so must all things follow. The Seed has evolved and grown Super-Conscious, assigning a new purpose to explore.' She swept her gaze. 'I cannot understand the details of this purpose yet, but I'm compelled to unravel its path through the practice of compassion. The reign of Senida is drawing to a close… the light will bleach her clean, and I can now see...'

Her eyes flashed. 'A great change is unfolding,' she shouted. 'Glory to this change.'

Lynium's face flickered like a weak signal. 'Great change,' he said in disbelief. His eyes darted nervously. 'Great change? This is crazy… some twisted trick.'

'No more tricks,' replied the Witch reassuringly. 'I'm eager to have you understand this, the Glorious Eternity has come.' She gestured out to The Seed. 'See how they turn from the darkness, see how they become healed.'

They peered through the layers and watched as one by one the army of Sirens, Warriors and Cyborg-Witches cracked open like concept eggs and spilled their beautified yolks. Everywhere, the manifest message was the same, sanity washed over madness, darkness shifted to light and violence settled into peace.

'I just can't believe it,' said Dreamweaver, 'I think it's really happening.'

Neris studied her vaporous instruments. 'It seems to be real, Peter,' she said. 'I'm picking up a rapid decline in all forms of evil; there's a paradigm shift sweeping The Seed.'

Lynium looked around despondently. 'You know, it's quite perverse really, but I'm almost disappointed that we didn't get to play it out.'

'I know what you mean, Lynium,' offered Dreamweaver. 'I'm sure I've been through this and it ended differently. He reached into his Spirit-Code and withdrew a thin cipher of time.

He shaped it into a book, opened it, then heard his own voice floating from the pages...

'This is where it all goes wrong for you, Storyteller,' Lynium shouted. 'This is where you find out that you're not what you thought you were. From now on, you're lost, I mean really lost. Up until this point it's all been a bit cosy, don't you think? Like some nice little adventure where the hero's working his way through this story... Well forget it!'

'I know how much you enjoyed the whole book thing with that damed kid,' Lynium shouted from thin air. 'So I thought I'd give you the bad news in a nice smart book. Go on, don't be shy! Pick it up! Have a read........'

Laughter imploded into thin air...............

Dreamweaver's mind continued scanning the pages of the book and was filled with sounds...images...feelings... He now saw Talis standing triumphant after her epic battle. But then he heard the chilling voice of Senida...

'Impressive.'

Talis turned slowly.

A sparkling disturbance moved in the air.

For a moment Talis was mesmerised by its brilliance and beauty. It seemed to hold her in a trance-like grip, drawing her into its fervent details.

Then very subtly and gently the dancing gleams coalesced into Senida.

There she stood, face like an abattoir of beautiful evils, her head circled by soft, catabolic flames; a vision stolen from myths. She wore a skin made of dancing filaments of light, the angelic illusion of living demoness.

She gracefully walked forward and stood in front of Talis.

'Impressive,' she said again in a melodic and feminine voice. Then added: 'What a pity it was all for nothing.'

Talis backed away. She moved her lips to speak, but nothing came out. Her mind seemed frozen.

'I think I have heard quite enough from you, so now you will remain silent,' said Senida impatiently. 'Do you want to know something?' she continued. 'I'm getting very tired and irritated by all this betrayal. First it's my own offspring, and now you, a Siren, the very creation I formed to promote my escape from the Circle.'

She walked up to Talis and held her chin. 'You've gone against all my design specifications.'

Talis tried to move, but found that she was paralysed.

'The other thing about all of this,' pondered Senida, 'is that I end up having to do everything myself.' She threw back her head, sending a stream of light into the air. 'I suppose that comes down to poor management.' She turned and looked down at the sizzling microdot that was once a great Warrior. Then scuffing it with her glowing foot, she added: 'But ultimately it returns to me.'

She lifted Talis into the air with one arm and let go, leaving her hanging in mid-air. The light withered still further, leaving stars dim and flickering. Her eyes were lit with violation. Arcs of beatific sparks drifted from Senida's hair, illuminating her merciless features.

She laughed, and a feminine chorus began singing faintly in unison with her laughter..... She gently looked up at Talis. A stream of torturous thoughts tore from her mind and melded into Talis' awareness...

'Oblivion will erase all your dreams,' whispered Senida. 'What good are dreams without a mind?'

Talis immediately felt the entirety of her mind being sucked into the torrent of darkness.

Senida lowered her gaze. 'There,' she said. 'That's better. All sucked out, nice and clean.'

And with a calm graceful movement, Senida blew Talis into a trillion pieces. She then turned her attention to the Witches that had betrayed her, bowing their heads to Talis. They stood frozen in her metaphysics, part of the same appalling thing; there was no chance of escape.

'Now hear this,' boomed Senida, in all her terrible magnificence. 'You have betrayed me so now there will be no end to your torment...no end.'

Her words brought an exclamation of horror from the Witches...

Dreamweaver closed the book. Tears streaming from his eyes.

He felt a hand touch his Soul-Pattern. He turned.

'I'm sorry, Dreamweaver,' whispered Neris. 'I know how special Talis was to you.'

Lynium nodded. 'Her sacrifice will not be in vain.'

'Yes, now we must do her justice,' said Dreamweaver calmly.

Neris went to take the book from Dreamweaver's hand, but he held it tightly. 'No,' he said firmly. 'No, Neris, I must do it, I know it has to be me.'

Lynium was breaking apart, pain moving through him. 'Senida will be in her Temple, she will be close to The Seed Singer,' he said softly. 'But before we go there, let's see if the book can still show us how the Story will unfold.'

Dreamweaver opened the book and lowered his eyes...the pages moved into his head and the Story took shape...

The transformed Cyborg-Witch calcified her transformation into the unfolding narrative like a particle of magic as they moved on past. Neris eased the thought-cloud towards Senida's Temple. They found their path through the scorching brilliance with feeling instead of fact, thought instead of time.

'I still can't believe it!' raged Lynium. 'A great change….???? I can never imagine Senida just handing this whole thing over?' His image faltered. 'Well….. can you?!… I swear to you that I'll…'

'Please, calm yourself, Peter,' urged Neris. 'Remember we still have work to do.'

He glanced back through the levels of alien consciousness to see the Witch expand into waves of joyful light. They moved past alien rivers, swollen in anticipation. A silence fell over them. They were now unsure of what lay ahead.

Then without warning, the great Spirit Temple loomed through their minds, its explosive towers sloping up in deep, feminine curves: endless dark-clad beauty. A ghostly spume caressed its roiling symmetries like the flesh of eternal damnation. This place was to misery what birth is to life. In Dreamweaver's mind it conjured images of impending sadness and doom; every thought of its construction playing some clever trick to confuse and frustrate. Many of the towers exploded with blinding darkness and rose both up and inwards in defiance of all things temporal. Its whole entropic presence was a deconstruction, oozing vile and blasphemous improbabilities.

Neris took the Thought-Cloud into a steep plunge, heading straight for the target. Down, down, down it went breaking through layer after layer of septic miracles.

'That's the most horrific structure I've ever seen,' said Dreamweaver.

'Wait until you're inside,' Lynium joked dryly.

'You know something, Lynium, you've got a really poor sense of humour.'

'I've picked up Senida in the vapours,' said Neris, 'She knows we're close.'

In a timeless instant, they flew to meet a flock of Cyborg-Witches, head on. Many of them now defined their presence with a melange of dancing glimmers, some had carved feminine light-bodies from their former malign structures. And at once they turned to embrace the three travellers, their iridescence filled with sympathy and knowledge. They surrounded them as if they were small children who needed protection. Then the most beautiful and formidable one of them spoke.

'Dreamweaver, you draw close to The Seed Singer, but there is still great danger,' she said. 'We will try to escort you past it so that you can complete your mission to liberate the Lost Souls.'

Dreamweaver sensed his fiction-destiny coursing through his construct being. He could almost imagine Senida's astounding spectacle, her touch, her endless, endless breath upon his lips.

The thought-cloud and its radiant escorts crossed the dramatic threshold as the full vision unfurled from the Temple of Spirit Technology. In a searing sheet of nightmares, Senida's raging form bled from the Temple, her feminine sulphur smeared with spiritual weapons.

Lynium stood at the front of the Thought-Cloud. Senida didn't take her eyes off him; she feasted on his torn yet measured danger. His powerful, outlaw drama became magnificent. A stream of legend bathed his face.

'So you've made this the final scene,' said Senida calmly.

She poured from a cloud of dreams.

'It's more than that…much more,' replied Lynium. 'Your ending is playing out before your eyes, Senida. The Whole realm moves against you, it's the medicine that comes to remove the pain.'

Two Warriors flew into the scene, flanking a cloud of Senida's approaching Sirens.

'You must know that you'll all be blasted into eternal pain,' said Senida, in calm confident tones. 'All of you…. The scene has arrived that knows no waking.' She hovered over her dark seraglio like a malignant angel. More and more Sirens gushed from Senida's body; a mournful, crushing song drifting from their lips.

'And so the end begins,' said Lynium as the Sirens' song moved around him. 'Our union created something of immeasurable beauty, and we have come now to reclaim that beauty from you. How such a miracle was made no longer matters; nothing matters any more, except its liberation.'

'Fine words from such a wretched creature,' hissed Senida. 'Such a pathetic structure dares to talk.'

'You're finished, Senida,' said Neris, trying to draw her into a strike position.

The song grew wild and alluring.

'You underestimate my powers,' countered Senida. She gazed at Dreamweaver, as several of her Sirens closed around him.

At once, Dreamweaver could barely believe what he saw. Senida appeared in his mind, immeasurably beautiful, fleshed with such vibrance. Her apparition was shaped as a woman, ripened, obscene, unsealed. Her paradox beauty eroticised his eyes as they feasted on her form. He could read no feelings as her image congealed with his thoughts, she was emptiness crammed full of forever. Her voice invited him, pulled him into her. He wanted to let go, needed to let go.

'Yes, it's good, you like it don't you?' Said Senida, laughing. 'It's too bad we will never have a chance to become better aquainted, Dreamweaver,'

Dreamweaver struggled through. 'I'll...get...over it.'

Neris edged around searching for her target.

Senida sensed Lynium move and swung her weapons around shouting in shocking patterns; she flared up like a stealth, her eyes possessed by anger, sweeping across The Seed in wild, staccato strokes, her licentious tongue flickering as she floated above. It was all Lynium required. He launched his damaged form from the helm of the Thought-Cloud, and before she could fully activate her power, he snatched Senida from her stratospheric orbit and they crashed down into the deep, conscious darkness below.

Dreamweaver surged past Neris, calling Lynium back before Senida could muster her force. 'Noooooooooo!!!!!!!!'

Lynium had played the ultimate hand and Dreamweaver's gesture came too late. Senida's power crawled through Lynium, tearing at his Soul with her striking systems; Lynium was powerless, unable to disengage himself now even if he'd wanted to. She lavished on his destruction as his mindless corpse surged into slurred slow motion and was gone.

With this, Neris transmuted into a gleaming black ghost; her ultimate weapon. She swooped towards Senida, a deadly gush – landing her devastating attack – piercing Senida's florid illusion. The felled Goddess shrieked and thrashed like a broken machine, but Neris would stop at nothing to destroy her.

Neris emerged as a shadow, but then solidified, staggered sideways and fell to her knees. Senida ejaculated everything she had into her, and Neris' form became a dance of hopeless spasms. And yet she refused to yield despite her ruined condition. Shafts of sunlight poured through her threadbare torso, knitting ghost-like patterns across the land. Her jet eyes puked rivers of burning cinnabar, as she moved away in a hail of particles.

Clouds of beautiful Witches swarmed across The Seed…

Through streams of Sirens and chaos, Neris pulled Dreamweaver from the Thought-Cloud towards a swarm of Black Ligh that nestled close to Senida's Temple.

'The end is set in motion…!' gasped Neris. 'Your destiny calls, Dreamweaver.'

A radiant Witch tore across the sky, shooting love from her eyes.

Senida constructed her valediction in a strange, thoughtless sound that swept like velvet through her lovely skull, and the Witch gasped as her gleaming visual tore apart.

As they fell into the Black Light, Dreamweaver saw an image of the Witch's perfect face showered with evil. She drank in her destruction like spring water, tearing her mind from Senida's realm. The gauzy remnant of her dazzling body embraced his eyes and the after-glow of her face was wild and full of passion. Breath and death had no pull on her Synthetic Soul.

Dreamweaver stretched out his hand as if to catch her energy.

'Leave it, Dreamweaver!' Neris insisted, pulling him down. 'It's too late for her, there's nothing we can do.'

'Why didn't you tell me!' shouted Dreamweaver.

'Lynium knew it was the only way to give me a chance,' insisted Neris. 'Nothing else can touch Senida.'

But now, despite Neris' zealous attack, Senida drew herself up, a Goddess resurrected. The enchantment of her beautified dream-flesh was bleached to a deadly white. Her fierce, exotic features smoldered in sensual static.

Her body bled hords of powerful Sirens that swarmed to deliver her destruction, but she slaughtered them with a contemptuous warp of her arm, evaporating them all in a glistening wave of torture. Senida staggered from this carnage, no longer effortless and magnificent. Her fine coating of illusion hung screaming in tatters.

'I will destroy you all….!' she yelled, her voice plunging to deep baritone slabs. 'Every last one of you… everything you are… all your dreams – everything!'

She turned her agonised eyes towards the Spirit-Code Temple. 'Dreamweaver….. I will destroy you… destro…. yed.' Her voice faltered and faded into the sensitive tissue of the void. 'You'll never make it to The Seed Singer,' she howled.

Overhead, Cyborg-Witches hovered like satellites, their ghostly machines hypnotising the air with their love. They were gathering in a pool of vibrant light to sweep away the darkness. The new pattern was in play and they would deliver its message.

Neris pulled Dreamweaver closer until they were locked like lovers. Her grip tightened around his arms and the ground beneath their feet rippled with Senida's anger. They stared into her once-lethal dynamics.

'Neris, it's no use, I know how this ends.' shouted Dreamweaver.

'I don't understand, Dreamweaver,' replied Neris.

He turned to her. 'I've told this story in the magic tongue...the detail has changed...but I know Senida destroys everything, nothing makes it.'

'Remember, Dreamweaver,' screamed Neris over the din. 'Remember what you have learnt and make it real.'

Radiance was departing from Senida. She was defaced, scrawled with carnivorous graffiti. Her magnificent Spirit-Code was no longer healing instantaneously; instead, whole sheets floated weightlessly from her body, crumbling like ancient papyrus.

She moved forward firing nightmares with one hand, keening her destruction through a smouldering mantra.

She smiled an arrogant smile.

'Your ambition can never be realised without my embrace, Dreamweaver!' she screamed, as the ground liquefied beneath her feet. 'It's over and you didn't make it through. The.... Seed is collapsing.... crumbling!'

The sky was filled with a terrible drone. Swirling darkness enveloped the land from hemisphere to hemisphere. Clouds of burning Spirits tore light from their eyes and threw it across the land. It spread through the action in bright monochrome strobes.

Neris stared at Dreamweaver. 'This didn't happen, it didn't happen. Only you can stop it...... it didn't happen!'

On cue, a cluster of Golden Warriors, arms spread out like ascending angels, flew above Senida. Their handsome dream-sculpted faces shimmered like moist spectres.

'Senida, it is time for you to join the light,' said the largest and most striking. 'We do not seek to destroy, merely to transform.'

Senida glanced up casually, smoldering like a stick of pernicious incense, 'You know it's useless, there will be no transformation.' Her voice had lost any trace of pain. Now it was full of sarcasm.

>>>>> Her sleek weapons swelled with deadly raptures. Her eyes bleached to a crisp, porcelain glint.

Neris snatched the book from Dreamweaver's hands. 'Break out Dreamweaver, it didn't happen, it didn't happen.'

Lynium held Dreamweaver close. 'It's OK, Storyteller, it didn't happen. 'Is this part of the Story...... God is this...????' screamed Dreamweaver.

'Take us down Neris, let's finish this off,' said Lynium, as he flickered violently.

Neris gently glided the Thought-Cloud towards Senida's Temple. And soon they were standing on the luminous hill, which led to their destination.

They slowly moved towards a crowd of angelic creatures: Warriors and Witches ever shifting, ever transforming. Two hovered like twin suns, their radiance filling the sky with melting sound. As the three travellers drew close, some of these new beings came to greet them, taking their hands to guide the last few steps. And it was then that they stared in shock, as the figure of Senida lay frozen in a gleam of time. Her extraordinary arms reached out to embrace a darkness that would never arrive. Her face was galvanised with eternal surprise.

Dreamweaver sensed his arrival, and more tears fell from his eyes. Lynium clasped his hand as they walked up to the entrance of the vast edifice.

'What the hell am I supposed to do in there?' asked Dreamweaver.

Lynium smiled. 'Only you will know, Storyteller,' he said. 'The Seed Singer said, the one that still lives must be the bridge, the one who comes from life will unlock my mind. Dreamweaver, you must find the method, you must find the key.'

'Why can't you both come with me?'

Again Lynium smiled. 'You don't know how much I want to, but my Spirit-Code's about to collapse if I don't get out soon, and besides, only you can complete the Story. Even Neris cannot survive in the Temple.'

Dreamweaver nodded. 'Well…' he offered. 'Seeing as I've come this far.'

He stared up at the entrance which stretched out before him. He perceived it as a vast paradox, built from the baseless materials of illusion. Slick, purposeful movement was everywhere across its surface. Unknown actions emerged from a dazzling sweep of alienised darkness; towers blazing with magic fed from its frame; visions seething with language and time fading like cloud-wreathed stories. There were thick lines of force – connected by sounds and silence – entering one part and leaving through another. It was more puzzle than portal.

Dreamweaver sat down cross-legged before the entrance, thinking. A thought came to him, *focus and learn to recognise who and what, in the midst of the chaos, is not chaos, then believe in this, make it vital and beautiful.*

He scanned the entrance until his mind focused on a microdot of order. Then, meditating on this as a yantra-structure, he slowly expanded it out until it gave order to more of the wild entropies. Soon he had fashioned a large area of smooth darkness to accommodate his body.

He turned to Lynium and Neris.

'I'm impressed, Storyteller,' said Lynium with a sly grin.

'I guess this is it,' said Dreamweaver.

There was a silent stillness…. They embraced.

'I'll miss you,' said Neris.

'Hey, I've a dinner date, remember to get some decent food.

He turned and stepped into the darkness.

23

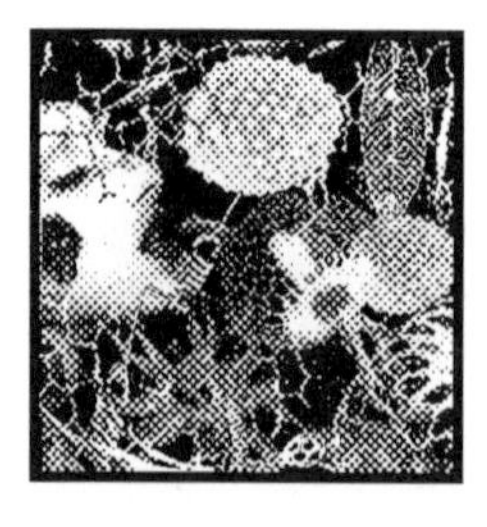

At once, a swirling fog enveloped him, images and sounds, movement.

A narrow path threaded through a landscape that grew knotted and wild. Dissolute sounds filtered through swaying, rhenium-leafed trees like faint pulses escaping from a hidden realm. A sharp, silver light bathed the scene, turning dust into splinters of diamond.

Dreamweaver smiled knowingly. *So we come to this*, he thought, *we come to this*. He traced the path as he'd done before. Somehow his mind had tried to conjure some vast spectacle for his final scene, yet part of him always knew it would end here.

He cast his mind back to the wonder of his first encounter with this place, the reflections, the hyper-detail of a world made from fiction. The slight wind brushed his face just as he remembered. This time he journeyed alone.

He stopped, and just listened to the sound of abundance; life eating life. Then he turned towards the clearing. Everything as before: frozen in a nether-time waiting for his return. He walked slowly into the dip, the lap of a giant.

And there it was in changeless perfection. The Shrine: the pigmy citadel. The smell of damp earth, the trees, the clouds, the sun. Now he understood more.

He sat down beside the crystal shrine and closed his eyes.

'You've almost completed your journey, Dreamweaver.'

Dreamweaver remained sitting, eyes closed. He smiled.

'It would seem so,' he said. 'But one can never be too sure of anything these days.'

She came and sat beside him. 'It didn't happen like the book, Dreamweaver.'

'What book are we talking about?'

'You must finish what you came here to do, Dreamweaver.'

He turned and looked at her face. The strong, tarnished beauty, the other-world eyes.

'Now there's a thing,' said Dreamweaver. 'What *did* I come here to do?'

'I don't understand...'

Dreamweaver reached into his pocket and removed the tiny, gold Soul-Casket. He wiped his hand across the eyes on the lid and watched it open. Then he gently removed the crystal figurine and held it in the palm of his left hand. Turning to the shrine, he dangled the tiny crystalline corpse over its centre. His eyes found the place where it would fit perfectly.

He turned and looked at her. 'Very beautiful,' he said.

She looked at him tenderly, almost bashful like a girl on a first date. 'You must release The Seed Singer, Dreamweaver,' she looked serious. 'There is no question... everything moves with this action.'

His eyes flashed. 'The Seed Singer, what is this Seed Singer... and what is this action?'

She gazed at him. 'Dreamweaver, you came here to realise the Pattern, to deliver the gift. In The Seed Singer all things are wiped clean and the pattern is complete.'

He smiled. 'In this Circle I've seen something of danger. I've seen how the concepts of good and evil are like a gentle breeze that ruffle the edges of clean-cut matter, and in the extreme they simply drop away; ripples that break the surface.... then gone... gone. The possibilities in this last act are endless. Are you the demon or the angel, am I the one who sets the destroyer free or am I the...' Then he laughed. 'In The Seed Singer's words, a key is a powerful thing, it can imprison or liberate with a simple flick of the wrist.'

Dreamweaver lowered the tiny figurine and it twinkled innocently like distant starlight. He sensed its power as it balanced on his fingers, waiting to find its purpose. 'And now what am I to be,' questioned Dreamweaver,' how does the Story end?'

He looked into her eyes...

'Now we begin...'